Amulet Books
New York

UP STAGED

BY DIANA HARMON ASHER

Page 282 constitutes a continuation of the copyright page.

Cataloging-in-Publication Data has been applied for and may be obtained from the Library of Congress.

ISBN 978-1-4197-4081-7

Text copyright © 2021 Diana Harmon Asher
Book design by Marcie Lawrence

Printed and bound in U.S.A.
10 9 8 7 6 5 4 3 2 1

Amulet Books are available at special discounts when purchased in quantity for premiums and promotions as well as fundraising or educational use. Special editions can also be created to specification. For details, contact specialsales@abramsbooks.com or the address below.

Amulet Books® is a registered trademark of Harry N. Abrams, Inc.

ABRAMS The Art of Books
195 Broadway, New York, NY 10007
abramsbooks.com

For Henry

Chapter 1

Pilgrim Feet

The front hallway of Hedgebrook Middle School has that slippery, early morning shine. I know by the end of the day it'll be back to its usual self, gray and grubby, marked up with black sneaker skids and gum pies. But now it's still polished and new and dotted with sunny spotlights. I weave a path around them, zigzagging my way to Mr. Hoover's Music Appreciation class.

Cassie's already waiting in the doorway, bouncing on her toes and waving me in. She has a new streak in her hair, bright blue to match her glasses. "Come on, Shira! The announcement, remember?"

Of course I remember. Mr. Hoover is really into announcements, and he's already let it slip that today's announcement is going to be about the school musical.

There's no reason why I should feel nervous. I have first-period math and Ms. Jablonski's evil pop quiz safely behind me. And I want to hear about the musical. I do. But something's making me hover in the doorway, until finally

Cassie has to practically yank me off my feet and pull me inside. We plop down in the third row.

"I *cain't* wait," Cassie says, putting on the goofy twang the kids used in last year's musical. "I want to get dressed up all *purty*."

"And dance with a *feller*," I say, then I throw in, *"Yeehaw."*

To be honest, it wasn't the best production in history. A cardboard cutout horse crashed down, barely missing the leading lady. And at the end, somebody stepped on the kid playing a farmhand who was supposed to be dead ("daid"). He screamed—much louder than a dead person ever would. It pretty much killed the drama.

Still, all the girls looked nice in their fluffy skirts, and the boys got to act all country, in their cowboy boots and hats. And, I admit, I wondered how it would feel to be up there in a costume, holding hands, singing, and taking a bow.

Mr. Hoover claps his hands for quiet. He's looking spiffy, as always, in a light green striped button-down shirt, pressed and tucked neatly into his khaki pants.

"Okay," he calls out. "Settle down now, people. I have an announcement!"

A cry of "whoo-whoo" comes from the other side of the room. I poke Cassie in the ribs.

"So, who came to see last year's musical?" asks Mr. Hoover.

Cassie and I raise our hands high, then look around

and lower them slowly. We're either the only two who went, or the only two uncool enough to admit it.

"Well, it was amazing," Mr. Hoover continues. "And this year's is going to be just as great. Now, enough suspense," he says, as if we're all on the edges of our seats. "I'm happy to announce—that this year—our school musical—will be—*The Music Man!*"

Cassie and I look at each other, not sure if this is good news or bad.

"This is such a great show. It's about a lovable con man and a small-town librarian . . ."

A drawn-out yawn comes from somewhere, and in the row behind us, a boy named Eric starts manufacturing a lineup of spitballs. The excitement is dwindling fast.

"Now, wait a minute!" calls out Mr. Hoover. "Keep listening. Because this year, we're holding auditions right here in music class!"

"Whuh?" says somebody, eloquently speaking for all of us.

"We'll still have after-school auditions, but I'm opening up our class today to anyone who wants to sing."

"Wait," says Cassie. "Now?"

"Yes!" answers Mr. Hoover, looking delighted. "And I *know* you're not ready. But that's the thing! There's no time to get nervous, no time to talk yourself out of it. I want everyone to take a chance. Even if you've never been in a show. Even if you're really, really shy."

When he says that last part, I swear he's looking right at me.

"What do we sing?" asks a girl named Frankie.

"Anything! 'My Country 'Tis of Thee' or 'America the Beautiful,' or . . . 'Uptown Funk' . . ." He pauses, clearly expecting a laugh, but there's silence. "Then come by Thursday after school to read a few lines, and you're done!"

Mr. Hoover sits down at the piano and waves an arm. "So, line up and let's go!"

Two boys in front of me start pushing each other, racing to hide under their chairs. Eric drops his spitballs and bolts dramatically for the door.

I sit still in my seat.

"Come on," says Cassie. "Let's get in line."

"Are you *kidding*?" I answer.

"Why not? You're in chorus. You have a nice voice."

"That's different. You don't have to audition for chorus."

"You know, when he said that shy part, he was looking right at—"

"I know," I snap.

"Listen," says Cassie, "we can't possibly be worse than that."

She's talking about Kevin Clancy. He's the kid who always wants to go first—scoliosis screening, hearing test, it doesn't matter. He's singing, "My Country 'Tis of Thee." At least I think that's what it is.

Mr. Hoover congratulates Kevin. "See?" he says. "It's easy." A few more kids start to get in line.

Cassie is standing, hands on hips. "What happened to this being the year you were going to stop being Shy Shira? The year you were going to stop blushing at every little thing?"

I take this as a reminder not to share secret goals with anyone, even if they are your best friend.

"We can go after school," I mumble.

"You know you won't," she says, and she's right. I won't. "Look, if you don't audition, I won't, either. Then neither of us will be in the show, and I'll never let you forget it. Ever."

I know she's not bluffing. She'll blame me, forever.

So, when she pulls me up out of my chair, I let her, even though my knees are shaking, and I feel like I might end up "daid" on the music room floor. And when she goes to the back of the line, I stand behind her, holding on to the thought that Cassie will go first, then I can bail.

Meanwhile, a group of boys cracks up through "She'll Be Coming 'Round the Mountain," and then a girl starts "My Heart Will Go On," but she loses her way and ends up in "I Will Always Love You." Somehow, Mr. Hoover knows to go along with her.

I'm fourth in line and it feels like feeding time for the butterflies in my stomach.

None of this makes sense. The kids who get the good parts are the ones who take acting lessons and dance class and go to Rising Starz Music Camp. The outgoing kids, the ones with confidence. Not kids like Cassie and me.

I stare at the floor, the singing and giggling a blur around me. But when I look up, Cassie isn't in front of me anymore. She's singing an enthusiastic and slightly off-pitch verse of "Oh My Darling Clementine." And then, before I can think of where to hide, it's my turn.

"'America the Beautiful'?" Mr. Hoover suggests, and before I can say no, please no, he plays a note and smiles.

Not every single kid is staring at me, but plenty are. I do a bobblehead move to catch the sweat droplet that's trickling down the back of my neck, but it's no use. That one's just the trailblazer. I know another is right behind it, and another and another.

I could burst into tears and run. But nothing marks you for life like crying in school, unless it's about a crush, or a breakup, or a B-minus, all subjects that have suddenly become cool to cry about this year. The only way out of this seems to be to sing and get it over with. But I promise myself, if I do this, if I get through this moment, then I'll never sing in front of anyone ever again. Because there are things that are Shira and things that are not Shira, and this is not a Shira thing.

My mouth has gone dry. I'm not sure if I'm breathing.

There's sweat behind my knees. I didn't even know knees could sweat.

It seems like Mr. Hoover has been holding that note forever. It hangs there, waiting for me. Mr. Hoover gives me a nod and plays it again. And finally, I start.

"Oh beautiful, for spacious skies, for amber waves of grain." I hear my voice, and it surprises me. Even though I'm shaking all over, it's not a disaster—yet. *"For purple mountain majesties . . ."* I make sure to say "mountain" and not "mountains," because Mr. Hoover always makes a huge deal that that's the right way. *". . . above the fruited plain."*

Something about the singing itself, the physical feeling of it, calms me down. It feels like taking a long stroke in a pool, feeling yourself propelled forward, in a smooth space where nobody can bother you. I sing, *"America, America,"* a little louder, because it feels good, the line of it, letting my voice free to go up there, and then come down softer on *"God shed his grace on thee."* One more line, one more line and I'll be done. *"And crown thy good with brotherhood, from sea to shining sea."*

I look at Mr. Hoover, and for a second I'm afraid he's going to want me to go on, to sing the second verse, which would be a disaster because I don't know all the words, just something about "pilgrim feet," which always makes me think of barefoot Puritans with big black hats and goofy cartoon toes.

But instead, he just drops his hands from the piano keys into his lap and smiles wide. "Thank you, Shira," he says. The room is quiet, and everyone is staring at me. I want to just run out of here, down the street, back home, up the stairs to my room, and never come out. I feel like I've just read the most embarrassing diary page ever written out loud to everybody. A diary I didn't even remember writing.

I run toward the door. I get as far as the second row, where my foot gets caught in a backpack strap. I manage to pull, drag, hop my way free and out to the hall, with the door crashing closed behind me. Then I drop down onto the floor, my back to the metal of somebody's locker, which I swear is rattling along to the pounding of my heart.

Inside, I can hear Mr. Hoover start up "The Star-Spangled Banner." And I listen as Dylan Scheiner butchers it, in at least three different keys.

Chapter 2

A Hat and a Mustache

On Friday morning, I dawdle my way toward the music room, stalling as long as I can. I tie my shoe. I check for texts. I free my hair from its scrunchie, then wrestle it back into something close to a ponytail.

I can always hope that when I get there, I'll find a sign reading:

PLAY CANCELED.

NO ONE HAS TO GET UP THERE ON STAGE AFTER ALL.

But no such luck. I can tell from the cluster of kids outside Mr. Hoover's room that the cast list is posted. Everybody's crowded around two little white sheets of paper tacked up on the bulletin board. Some kids are on tiptoes, others push forward, all trying to get a look. A kid named Sean lets out a whoop and squirts out of the crowd like a watermelon seed. He runs into the music room and comes out with two books that say "The Music Man" on them in purple letters. Then he races down the hall to spread the news. A lanky girl named Delilah shouts, "Mrs. Shinn!" and raises her arms in triumph.

I consider ducking into the girls' room to buy a little more time, but I put that idea away when I see Monica Manley and Melinda Croce prance in there shoulder to shoulder, whispering and giggling. I choose to avoid being in enclosed spaces with eighth graders in general, and Monica and Melinda in particular. And there's no use waiting. If there's a mirror involved, it won't be a short visit for Monica.

"Shira!" I turn and see Cassie running toward me. Her backpack is bouncing like a rodeo rider hanging on for dear life. "Come on! What are you waiting for?"

I wish I knew. I'm not even sure what I'm hoping for. But whatever it is, I need another minute before I'm ready to see it dashed to pieces.

Cassie shakes her head and runs toward the crowd. She plunges in, but I stay back, thinking. I survived the singing tryout. Somehow, I managed to stumble through the reading audition, but only because one of the monologue choices was Sally Brown's speech from "It's the Great Pumpkin, Charlie Brown!" which I watched about a hundred times when I was five.

All I have to do now is go up and look at the cast list.

I take a deep breath, count to ten, and creep up to the

back of the crowd. Then I let the new arrivals jostle me forward and carry me in gradually, like a rock washing up on shore.

Someone has crossed out the "BROOK" in Hedgebrook and written in "HOG." No surprise. Then, listed first, are the leads:

HOG!
HEDGE~~BROOK~~ MIDDLE SCHOOL FALL MUSICAL

Meredith Willson's *THE MUSIC MAN*

Professor Harold Hill   **Paul Garcia**

Marian Paroo   **Monica Manley**

So that explains Monica's whispers and giggles. It makes sense. She's the obvious choice for the lead, an eighth grader who takes voice and dance lessons. I've even heard some of the girls say in awed tones that she auditions for commercials in "The City." That's New York City. And anything that happens in "The City" has to be way better than whatever we do here in Hedgebrook.

I muster my courage and scan the first page, looking for my name. I see the mayor's wife—that's Mrs. Shinn—and someone or something called Amaryllis. I see Cassie's name on the second page. She's a townsperson. There are River

City Ladies and band members and someone named Ethel Toffelmeyer. But my name isn't next to any of those roles. It's not anywhere.

I should feel relieved. I promised myself I'd never sing in front of anyone ever again, and now I won't have to.

But Cassie has been telling me all week how Mr. Hoover's face lit up when I sang, how I sounded really good, and how I could surprise everyone and get a big role. And when someone keeps saying something, even if it's crazy, a little part of you starts to half believe it. Or maybe hope it. Or maybe be terrified of it. Or maybe all three.

I look at the second page one last time, and then, far down, at the very end, I see it:

The Barbershop Quartet

Mr. Ewart Dunlop	Vijay Mehta
Mr. Olin Britt	Jason Chen
Mr. Oliver Hix	Felix Owen
Mr. Jacey Squires	Shira Gordon

"Hey, Shira," says a boy I recognize from math class. "You're a guy."

I pretend not to hear, because there's no point denying it. It's right there in black and white.

"My mom made me watch the movie," this kid goes on. "There are these four dudes with matching hats and mustaches who sing all the time. '*La-la-la*,'" he demonstrates, just in case I don't know what singing is. "You're totally playing a guy."

I stare at my name and try to come up with some other explanation: Maybe it's Ms. Jacey Squires. Maybe I'm somewhere else on the list, and this is just a mistake. I look again, but there's only: "Mr. Jacey Squires . . . Shira Gordon."

I tell myself it's not so bad. It could be a lot worse. I could be playing the rear end of a mule, or an old hag with missing teeth, or the town drunk. I could be asked to die a horrible death or dance in a tutu. It's not that unusual for a girl to play a boy's part. And it's not like I'm some super girlie type who only talks about nail polish and shoes. When I was little, my dolls sat on the shelf while I played with my toy dinosaurs, and I loved my Captain America Halloween costume in third grade. Still. It's not third grade anymore. It isn't even sixth. This is seventh grade, when people notice you. For all the wrong things.

Cassie was right. I did want to be in the show. In the back row, maybe. A villager among villagers. Wearing a pretty costume. But there won't be any fluffy skirt for me. No ruffles. No frou-frous. Not a single, solitary frou.

There's a sign in big letters telling us to pick up our scripts and scores in the music room, but I don't. My ears are starting to burn, and I know soon I'll be in full Shira blush mode. I turn away from the list and look for Cassie.

"Good luck with that," chuckles the "la-la" kid as he runs down the hall—probably on his way to spread the word to the whole seventh grade that Shira Gordon is playing a guy.

Chapter 3

Radar

Cassie is waiting for me down the hall.
"You've said a million times, nobody here knows you exist.
They're not even going to notice."

It isn't much of a compliment, but maybe Cassie is right.
Maybe the fact that I'm practically invisible in this school
will finally work to my advantage.

There's still a small crowd near the music room,
flipping through their scripts and checking the list for their
friends, but most kids are slamming lockers and running
to make first period. Maybe Ms. Jablonski will finally hand
back that pop quiz and make my day a perfect ten. Cassie
walks next to me, still talking. I walk next to her, still sulking.

"Come on, Shira. It's not a big deal."

A kid passes us, then he turns around, walking backward
and pointing a finger at me. "Hey, Shira," he says. "Not
fair. About the play . . ." I stay hopeful for about two seconds. "That's the part I wanted."

As he blats out a self-congratulatory laugh, two eighth-
grade girls collapse in giggles.

"See?" I say. "They make it a big deal. They wait for anything different, any sign of weakness."

"Then don't show weakness. Stand up and take it like a—"

I glare at her. I'm not really in the mood for Cassie's sense of humor right now.

"Look. I'm a lowly townsperson. You have a real part, with a name and songs. Who cares if you wear a mustache?"

"It puts me on their radar," I say.

"Whose radar?"

"Everybody's. The whole school's."

"So? Maybe it's time for you to be on somebody's radar. Picture it. You've been Miss Nobody all these years. Now you can step into the spotlight. Wow everybody with your incredible talent."

"I don't want to wow anybody. I don't want to be in any spotlights. I didn't even want to audition."

"But you were fantastic! Come on, Shira. You know you want to be in the show."

"Do not," I lie.

Now it's Cassie's turn to glare.

Suddenly, we hear running footsteps coming from the direction of the music room. I turn and see a kid practically flying around the corner. He tries to stop, but his sneakers won't hold. His arms are whirling around like a windmill, his hands grabbing at nothing, and he comes sliding to a stop in the middle of the floor with a skid and a *thunk*.

Somehow, those eighth-grade girls are passing by again, magically reappearing. They half cover their mouths and scrunch up their shoulders in that perfect pretend-to-stifle-a-laugh-but-not-really motion.

The running boy is halfway up on his feet when another kid breaks away from his friends and pokes the boy's shoulder just hard enough to send him back to the tiles. The girls, of course, think that's hysterical.

Oddly enough, this boy on the floor hardly seems to notice. He just looks up at me and says, "You're Shira, right?"

"Um, yes," I say. He doesn't seem like the type, but I prepare myself for an offer of a jock strap or a lesson in the use of urinals. If even the marginal kids are going to give me a hard time, I'm really in trouble.

But instead, he just gets up carefully and brushes himself off like it's all in a day's work. He's hardly taller than me, with curly hair and a smooth, young-looking face.

"I was looking for you," he says. "I'm Paul."

"Okay," I say.

"No, I mean, Paul Garcia. Professor Harold Hill." He's smiling. He looks enthusiastic. The kind of enthusiastic that's the kiss of death in school.

"Well, congratulations," I say, but when his smile droops, I realize that it sounded a little like when you say "congratulations" as a put-down, so I try to pep up my delivery and say, "Really. Congratulations."

"Thanks," says Paul, his smile safely back in place.

"I'm Cassie," she says. "Townsperson."

"Nice!" says Paul happily. "Are you excited?"

"Yes! Aren't we, Shira?" Cassie gives me a light shove with her elbow, and I manage a half-hearted smile.

I look Paul over, but I can't figure him out. Something marks him as the kind of kid who doesn't quite know the codes. The kind who wears red on blue day or jeans on shorts day, even though it's not written anywhere that it IS blue day or shorts day. But some kids know, and some kids don't. He's definitely in the don't category. But what I can't figure out is if he doesn't get it, or if he doesn't care.

"Shira." Paul's still smiling. "Mr. Hoover wants to see you."

"Mr. Hoover? Why?"

"I don't know. He just said to tell you to stop by after lunch."

I look at Cassie. She makes a beats-me face. It occurs to me that this could be good news. Maybe some weird glitch in the computer program put my name next to Mr. Jacey Squires, and that's not my part at all. Maybe I'm a townsperson like Cassie, or a River City Lady.

"Okay," I say, feeling a twinge of hope. "Thanks."

"He says he can write you a late pass," Paul adds.

"Speaking of late." Cassie's starting down the hall. "I

have to get to science. If I'm the last one in, she'll give me detention and make me clean the meal worm habitat." She gives a little shudder, then she turns and trots off.

I take a few steps toward first-period math. Paul calls after me, "See you at rehearsal!"

"Um, sure," I say, even though right now, I'm not sure about very much at all.

Chapter 4

A Grubby Old Ball

After lunch, I head over to see Mr. Hoover.
The hallway is quiet, except for a woman standing in the doorway of the music room. She's in fit-mom clothes: three-quarter-length tights, a sleeveless workout shirt, and sneakers. She's gesturing with a plastic Starbucks cup, a long straw pointing up out of the lid.

"Well, see what you can do," she's saying.

Mr. Hoover's voice is coming from inside. "I will, Mrs. Manley. But I wish Monica had told me this in advance."

"Oh, whatever. All I'm saying is, she can't be expected to miss opportunities. Her future might be made in the very next audition."

"I understand. But it's just not common for us to allow absences—"

"Well, Monica is hardly common, is she, Mr. Hoover?"

"Of course not," he answers.

"And this production is lucky to have her."

"We're lucky to have a lot of talented young people. Our Harold Hill—"

"She's going to wipe those other kids off the stage," Mrs. Manley says.

"Well, no, no, I wouldn't say that."

"Well, you can't, can you?" She gives a little chuckle. "But anyway. I'm sure you'll work out some kind of backup. I'll leave it to you."

She doesn't wait for an answer. She takes a few brisk, sneakered steps in my direction, taking a long sip of her iced whatever-it-is. I catch a glimpse of her name tag as she passes me: Dora Manley, SPAM.

When she's a safe distance down the hall, I creep up to the door of the music room. I take one more look at the cast list, and seeing that nothing has changed, I poke my head inside.

Mr. Hoover is sitting at his desk. His jacket is hanging neatly on the back of his chair. A picture of his husband is propped up between a statue of Beethoven and a tall pile of songbooks. He's rubbing his head, thinking, so I knock lightly on the door and Mr. Hoover looks up.

"Shira!" he says. He looks almost gleeful to see me. Or maybe just relieved that it's not Monica's mom. He jumps up and takes two books off the top of the piano—a gray softcover and a bigger one with an orange cover. "You didn't pick up your script and your score." So, no mistake. No computer glitch. Just, here's your script, Mr. Jacey Squires.

He's holding the books out to me, but I don't reach for them.

"Don't tell me you're having second thoughts," he says.

Second, third, fourth . . . I'm thinking.

He puts the books down and pulls over a chorus chair. "Sit down. Let's talk."

Mr. Hoover's desk chair makes a little puff sound when he sits. The alligator on his shirt smiles at me, baring its little white teeth. Everything about him looks as ordered and cheerful as I am unraveled and confused.

"Shira," he says. "You must be wondering why I've given you this part."

Oh no, not at all, I want to say. *It's what I've always dreamed of.*

"Look," he says. "I know this is all new. And I wouldn't have even considered giving you a role like this if I didn't know what a smart, talented, mature young person you are."

I'm squirming in the cold plastic chair, feeling un-smart, un-talented, and incredibly un-mature.

"Shira, I was so proud of you! You had such a great audition. I considered you for Amaryllis, or one of the River City Ladies. But the barbershop quartet is such a special part of *The Music Man.* You sing 'Lida Rose,' and 'Goodnight, Ladies'! The harmonies are tremendous."

I've never heard of "Goodnight, Ladies," I still don't know what an Amaryllis is, and I don't think harmonies can be tremendous.

"Have you ever heard a barbershop quartet?"

"No," I say.

Mr. Hoover shifts forward in his seat. "It's four singers—bass, baritone, first and second tenor. The second tenor sings the melody. That's called the lead, but the first tenor sings the upper harmony. That's your part. We have Vijay, Felix, and Jason, who are really good singers. But without a first tenor . . ." He shakes his head. "We need someone to hold the quartet together."

What comes out of my mouth is what I've been thinking this whole morning. "But, why me?"

"Because you're a musician, Shira. I can hear it in chorus. You're always right there. Right on pitch. The other kids follow you."

I don't know what he's talking about. "I just read the notes," I say.

Mr. Hoover smiles. "Lots of people can read music. It's more than that," he says. "But you'll see. This is a great part. And trouser roles are an old tradition—women playing men. There's Cherubino in *The Marriage of Figaro*, and Orfeo in *Orfeo ed Euridice* . . ."

Okay, so I think he's talking opera. I need to get out of here, fast.

Mr. Hoover's face is so full of excitement. I know he thinks he's offering me something special. Like when a dog comes bounding over with a grubby old ball, and he drops it at your feet. He's all happy and proud and he expects you to be thrilled with his gift to you, but all you see is a grubby old ball.

I like Mr. Hoover. He's one of the few teachers here who seems to actually want to be spending time with us. It makes me feel guilty that I'm going to have to tell him no, I've changed my mind. I don't want to be in the show. But before I can say anything, he slaps his hands on his knees, jumps up, and grabs those books again. "Just do this for me: Take the script and the music score. Look them over. Listen to the music." He holds the books out, and this time I take them. I just can't bear to disappoint him. He puts a hand softly on my shoulder. "We really need you, Shira."

Mr. Hoover writes out a late pass. "You better get to class, or I'll get in trouble." I don't know how a teacher can get in trouble, but, okay.

I take my pass and head to English. I walk slowly and think it over. All I have to do is sing first tenor, wear a mustache and hat, and have every pair of eyes in the school watching me.

No big deal. No big deal at all.

Chapter 5

Cooties

"You're playing a boy," says my little sister when I get home. So even the fourth grade has heard about it. The way news spreads around here, I might as well be living in Tincup, Colorado, population forty-five. Mom is sitting at the kitchen table with her laptop.

"What's this I hear about you being in a play?" she asks. So much for my plan not to tell her so she won't be disappointed when I quit.

"Mr. Hoover wants me to be in *The Music Man*," I explain. "But I can still say no."

"*The Music Man*?" She puts down her pen. "I *love The Music Man*. Robert Preston. Shirley Jones, Hermione Gingold . . ."

"You mean Hermione Granger?" asks Sophie.

"No, I mean Hermione Gingold," she answers in her there-was-a-world-before-you-were-born tone. "She's in *Gigi*, too." Sophie and I exchange a look. "And Opie, the one who was in *Happy Days*, played the little boy . . . what's his name . . . Winthrop!" Sometimes my mom goes into these connect the dots memories from another planet and we just have to wait until she's finished.

"Is that the part you got?" asks Sophie. "Winthrop?"

"No," I say. "I'm in the barbershop quartet."

"The barbershop quartet? Oh Shira, that sounds like fun."

"Mom," I say, "I'd be playing a guy with a mustache."

She stops to think about that for about a tenth of a second. "Oh, don't worry," she says, "you'll look adorable. And besides, there's a long tradition of girls playing boys. It's in Mozart all the time."

Did Mr. Hoover give her a call while I was at school, or do all adults have a secret trove of information about things like this?

"And Shakespeare," she adds. "Look at *Twelfth Night*."

"That was way before they invented middle school, Mom," says Sophie.

"So, who's playing Marian the Librarian?" my mom asks.

"Marian the Librarian?" repeats Sophie.

"Monica Manley," I say.

"No surprise there," Mom mutters. "With all those private lessons I would hope she'd get the lead. Her mother talks about her like she's the next Lady Gaga. And who's playing Harold Hill?"

"A kid named Paul Garcia," I say.

"Is he hot?" asks Sophie.

"Hot?" says my mother. "Sophie, you're in fourth grade. What happened to 'cute'?"

Sophie just ignores her. "Well, is he? Or is he one of those theater dweebs?" She turns to Mom. "That's like, a nerd, a loser . . ."

Mom nods. "We used to say they had cooties."

"Thanks," I say. "That's helpful."

"I'm not saying he *does*. I'm just telling you that's what we called it."

"So?" asks Sophie.

"He's neither. I mean, I don't know. I just met him today."

"Did Cassie get a part?" asks my mother.

"She's a townsperson," I answer.

"Female?" asks Sophie.

"Yes," I say, hissing a little bit.

"So, you're in the show together!" says Mom. "Shira, that's wonderful."

Mom looks like she could burst with joy. She already has me up there, taking a bow. It's what mothers do. At least what my mother does. I have to get out of here before she gets tears in her eyes. Hopeful tears. Maybe-Shira's-ready-to-come-out-of-her-shell tears.

I go for the stairs.

"Much homework?" my mother calls after me, trying to keep things normal.

"Social studies project," I answer. As I climb up the stairs, I can practically feel the rays of hopefulness beaming up from behind me.

"Shira!" calls Mom, and I stop midway. "Congratulations, sweetie." And before I can get out of hearing range, she follows with the dreaded, shaky-voiced, "I'm so proud of you."

I close my eyes and take a deep breath, wondering how I'm going to back out of this now that my mother's hopeful seedlings have been so tenderly planted.

At the top of the stairs, I turn left and climb the three little steps up to my room. I love my room. The carpet is light blue and extra soft, and the ceiling slopes down so I feel like I'm tucked into a camper's lean-to. On the side wall, there's a full-sized window, but in front there's a tiny one that's shaped like a half-moon, pinched at the edges. It's called an eyebrow window. I can look out, but except for a few birds and an occasional squirrel, nobody can see in.

I pull the script and the score out of my backpack, plop them on my bed, and sit beside them. The score is thick, with an orange cover. It has the music and lyrics, even the piano part. The script has all the characters' lines. I open it to a random page, where Harold is talking to his friend Marcellus. He's saying that Harold won't have much luck getting Marian the Librarian to like him. It sounds like she's kind of a snob and a little stuck-up. I flip to another scene where the mayor's wife, Mrs. Shinn, is leading the other ladies in a dance, and another one where Harold and Winthrop are singing a song called "Gary, Indiana." Then near the end, there's a scene with Harold and Marian on a footbridge. At the end, the stage directions say "They kiss." I wonder if that's even allowed in a middle school production.

Mr. Hoover mentioned a song with "goodnight" in it, so I put down the script and try YouTube. I find a song called "Goodnight, My Someone." When it starts, I realize it's not the barbershop quartet singing, it's Marian. But it's such a pretty melody, I keep listening. It's the kind of song that sounds familiar, like you've heard it somewhere before. Marian is saying goodnight to her "someone," because she doesn't know who it is yet. It's a little corny but kind of romantic. I feel that way sometimes. Like there's someone or something out there waiting for me, and I just don't know what it is yet.

There's a knock on the door. It's Sophie. "You gonna do it?" she says through the door.

I don't answer. Instead, I put on my earphones. Usually, I'll put on Spotify—which I've managed to convince I'm a typical twelve-year-old girl with typical twelve-year-old tastes. But today, I listen to Marian singing about her someone. It's a waltz, really. I put one arm out to the side, and with the other, I hold my imaginary partner, not too close, just close enough. And I think, maybe Marian's not stuck-up at all. Maybe she's just unsure of herself and hard to get to know. Maybe just a little sad. Or shy.

And soon I'm twirling, around and around, waltzing to Marian's song about wishing and waiting and imagining, safe in my room, alone on my soft, blue carpet.

Chapter 6

Cartoon Chicken

I give myself the weekend to decide. I've learned that sometimes things look clearer after a good night's sleep.

I've also learned that sometimes they don't.

At least there's something to distract me over the weekend. My first Bar Mitzvah party.

There are a lot of Jewish kids at Hedgebrook, so that means lots of Bar and Bat Mitzvah parties. It's a tradition for Jewish boys to have a Bar Mitzvah and girls to have a Bat Mitzvah near their thirteenth birthday. Tyler is one of the oldest kids in the grade. I'm one of the youngest, so my Bat Mitzvah won't be until next September.

The ceremony is in temple on Saturday morning. When it's your turn for a Bar or Bat Mitzvah, you get to read a part of the Torah and sing the blessings. It's all in Hebrew and it's really beautiful. Then you talk about what you just read and tell everyone what you've learned now that you're thirteen and practically an adult.

Then most kids have a big party.

Some kids get invited to every single one. I know because I see them comparing their invitations and save-the-date cards in the cafeteria. Sometimes glitter falls out of the envelope all over the cafeteria floor. Tyler Glass's is the first—and only—Bar Mitzvah I've been invited to. Not that I'm surprised.

I know "shy" doesn't get a lot of press these days. From a distance, it probably doesn't seem much different from being quiet or calm or peaceful. Or boring. But for me, it's like the inside of you wants to be talking and laughing, in the middle of everything, sitting at the table that's having so much fun, but a piece of you won't let you.

When I was little, my mom tried to find me the perfect playmate. First, she invited a quiet girl named Emily over, but it turned out that two quiet kids just made things doubly quiet. Then she tried the outgoing girls like Becky Treetorn, who talked nonstop about her doll collection while her Rottweiler, Jagger, waited outside in the hallway, panting. She said he was more afraid of me than I was of him, but I didn't see why he would be afraid of a little kid like me, while I had plenty of reasons to be afraid of him—teeth and drool being just two of them. It was not a successful playdate.

I tried to fit in, but all the girls wanted to play those hand-clap games where you sing songs over and over. Some of the girls slapped really hard and others had wet, sweaty palms. Then there were the boys, who rammed their trucks into each other making *rrrrrr* noises. With every playdate, I was happier and happier staying in my room, by myself.

Cassie is the one exception. When she moved to town in fifth grade, I knew right away we had things in common. Things that made us different from most of the girls at school, like only saying things after our heads had filtered them through at least once and not giggling unless something was verifiably funny.

Cassie's parents are divorced, so she lives with her mom, around the corner from me. I think I would feel bad if I were Cassie, but she doesn't let the divorce get her down. She once told me that sometimes it's the obstacles that can make you appreciate the good things. One day, the sun was shining down through the trees in these milky-looking shafts. And Cassie pointed out that there were all these little dust particles floating around, and we probably wouldn't have even noticed that shaft of light if the dust particles weren't there.

So, I try to put all these specks of dust about the show out of my head and find the shaft of light. Maybe I'll find it at Tyler Glass's Bar Mitzvah party.

The Bar Mitzvah service was this morning at Temple Beth Shalom. Most kids don't even bother going to the service, but I feel better knowing I've put in some temple time. Cassie would've come, but she had a phone call scheduled with her dad.

Tyler did a pretty good job reading from the Torah and talking about it. I'd say he lucked out with his Torah portion.

He got the story of Noah and the flood and talked about pet adoption—kind of a stretch, but nobody's expecting a real sermon or anything.

My mom told me that her whole Torah portion was about leprosy. Good luck with that.

Hardly any other kids were at temple, just one boy who I recognized from math and about six of Tyler's soccer buddies, who were squirming around in the back row where one of the ushers had to shush them a million times. And as I was leaving, I thought I saw Paul Garcia sitting way up front.

But now it's seven o'clock and it's time to get ready for the party. I pull out the dress my mom helped me choose. It's light blue with wavy stripes of green and pink and not nearly as flattering as it looked in the store. I look a little like a swirly rainbow Popsicle.

"A part in the play and a Bar Mitzvah party," my mother says when I come downstairs. "This is just so exciting." Those tears are glinting in her eyes again.

"At least for the Bar Mitzvah I get to wear a dress," I mutter, tugging it down in back. It didn't seem this short in the store, either.

My dad tosses the car keys in the air, catching them in his right hand with a flourish. "Your chariot awaits," he says, and I follow him to the car. I get in, trying to keep my dress from riding up too high.

We pick up Cassie, who's put in her brand-new contact lenses. She sits in the back, where she's alternately blinking and squinting out the front windshield. Neither of us has ever been to the Sunnydale Country Club, and as we pull into the driveway, a line of cars is stretched out for what seems like a mile. "You think Tyler invited the whole grade?" she asks.

"He must've," I say. "*We're* here, right?"

We crawl forward until we see the front of the building. A man with a rounded English-style hat and a white scarf is directing traffic. He escorts people out of their cars, then his red-jacketed helpers jump behind the wheel and roar away like they're never coming back.

"Whoa," says my dad, "valet parking. Pretty fancy." The parade of sedans is interrupted every few cars by SUVs that spit out four or five kids onto the curb and drive away. When it's our turn, the Englishman slides open our minivan door. Cassie climbs out, and after a peck on the cheek from my dad, I hop out to meet her.

"I'll come get you at . . . What's the pickup time?" my dad calls through the window.

"Midnight, sir," says the Englishman.

"Midnight? Are they crazy? These kids aren't even thirteen." The Englishman just shrugs, like he's seen a lot of crazier things. "What do you think?" my dad asks me. "Eleven?"

"Sure, Dad," I say. I know most kids would argue,

pleading for that last hour, but the truth is, eleven o'clock sounds just fine to me. If it's like every other party, I'll end up with no one to talk to except Cassie, counting down the minutes until it's over. Sometimes it comes in handy to have reasonably uptight parents.

We wave goodbye and walk up the stairs into the front hallway, following a lady in shoes with about fourteen-inch heels and the pointiest toes I've ever seen. I can practically hear her toes screaming in there.

Following a sign that says "KIDZ PARTY," we turn away from the room that smells like charbroiled steak, into another room that smells like movie popcorn and fried chicken. It's a maze of flashing lights, with rap music pounding from the DJ's speakers. A super-fit Dance Lady–Hostess-type person bounces by, doing an exaggerated arm-pump-neck-thrust dance that makes her look like a cartoon chicken.

We pass a dripping chocolate fountain and a table where a bartender is making drinks in a blender. A Hawaiian-shirted, ponytailed guy hands each of us a glowing necklace, and before I can even say thank you, he's gone.

To our right, I spot my lab partner, who nearly set our table on fire twice. To our left is the girl with a locker above mine who manages to step on me at least once a day. Both look perfect, in their spaghetti-strap dresses, with their shining hair and sparkling eye makeup.

"Hey," a voice says.

I turn and see that "la-la" kid from yesterday.

"Left your mustache at home?" he asks. The other boys at his table crack up at his brilliance, congratulating him on his joke of the year.

I realize how much I don't want to be here. I feel tears coming to my eyes. Humiliation kind of tears. Looking like a Popsicle kind of tears. But Cassie pulls me over to the blender bar, and I try to picture that kid shrunken to ant-size and thrown in there, getting whirred and spun mercilessly around in the goo.

Our pink and yellow slushies slop over the sides of our plastic cups. We hold them at arms' length, in our not-at-all-slinky dresses and not-styled hair, and stand there, our neon glow rings shining like reject signs around our necks, with nowhere to go.

Eleven o'clock? Try eight fifteen.

But then, through the speeding disco lights, we see someone waving.

"Is he waving at us?" Cassie asks me. She's blinking and squinting some more. I don't know if those contact lenses have a future.

"Who would be waving at us?" I say. Now I squint, too. "I think . . . I think . . . it's . . . Paul."

"Paul Garcia?" asks Cassie.

"Yup," I answer. "Professor Harold Hill."

Chapter 7

Telling Fortunes

"Should we go?" Cassie asks as we look around at the other options we don't have.

"I guess," I say.

Paul is waving with both hands now and he's climbed up on a chair to make sure we see him.

"He's energetic, isn't he?"

"Yeah," I answer. "A little overboard, you think?"

"Enthusiastic," says Cassie. I nod a sad nod.

We make our way through the tables. We pass a woman with a crystal ball who's walking around telling fortunes, but nobody seems interested. By the time we get to Paul's table, he's back in his seat.

"Hey, Shira," he says to me like we're old friends. He turns to Cassie. "Hi again. We met in the hallway yesterday."

"I remember," says Cassie, kindly leaving out the fact that he was sprawled out on the hallway floor at the time.

The boy next to Paul is sitting with a plate full of chicken fingers and fries, slumped down in his chair. His chubby hands cover his ears, his eyes are closed, and his nose is wrinkled up.

"Do you know Jason?" asks Paul, and I shake my head. "Jason Chen." When Paul taps him on the shoulder, he opens his eyes and looks surprised to see us.

"Oh," Jason says. "Sorry." He points one finger at the DJ and yells, "How much longer?"

"We just got here," shouts Paul, and then to us, "He hates Bar Mitzvahs."

"Not the temple part. I like the temple part," Jason says. Now I realize that he's the kid I saw at the service. "I like the Torah blessings. I almost have the first one memorized."

"Wow," says Cassie. "How many Bar Mitzvah services have you been to?"

"Just one other one. But I like the melody. I googled it." He takes one hand off his ear long enough to pop a fry into his mouth. "I just hate the party part. Too loud. Too crowded."

"So why did you come?" I shout.

"My mom said I had to. She wants me to be more social."

There's finally a break in the blasting music and Jason's words boom out. A few giggles come from the next table. Jason shrugs, uncovers his ears, and takes a handful more fries.

"I've been to two others," says Paul. "But the first one

was my next-door neighbor, and the second one, her parents knew my parents."

Jason nods. "That's how I got my other one, too."

"Hey," says Cassie, "aren't you in the barbershop quartet with Shira?"

"Yup," says Jason. "With Vijay and Felix."

I toss Cassie a frosty look. I'm not in the barbershop quartet yet. Not until I give Mr. Hoover an answer.

But before I can say anything, the disco ball comes to life, giving everyone a case of traveling green and purple pox. And even though I didn't think it was possible, the music starts back up even louder than before.

"Everybody out on the dance floor!" calls the Dance Lady. Chairs scrape and tables empty as kids rush out there. The ponytail guy gets them all in a conga line. At our table, Jason's hands are back on his ears and he looks like he was just asked to dive into a pool of barracudas. Cassie stares at her drink, twirling her slushie straw in a circle. I entertain myself by making fists and feeling my sticky slushie fingers peel away from my palms one by one.

"Isn't anybody going to dance?" Paul calls across the table.

Jason just shakes his head.

"Why not?"

"Because we'd look stupid!" he shouts. "Like them," he adds, with a tilt of his head.

"He has a point," says Cassie.

Paul looks out at the crowd. "We wouldn't look any stupider than anybody else."

"The difference is," shouts Jason, "they don't know how stupid they look, and we would."

I look out at the dance floor. Everyone does look pretty silly. Most of the girls are clustered together, waving their arms and wiggling their hips, watching themselves in a mirrored wall. The green and purple dots have morphed into blue and white streaming beams and then to traveling multicolored stars. Most of the boys are jumping around, spinning in circles, kicking each other from behind.

I settle into my chair, content to sit this out. At least I'm not alone. I watch the kids on the dance floor, a mess of limbs and twisting shapes.

But in the middle, there's one boy who doesn't look stupid at all. He's watching the Dance Lady and following her moves perfectly. Every few steps he brushes his light brown hair away from his eyes. His white shirt turns blue, then red, then yellow as lights and flashing stars wash over him. I try not to stare, but I can't help it.

The Dance Lady notices him, too, and she pulls him from the crowd to be her partner. I watch him out there, next to her, looking somehow athletic and easy at the same time.

Clap-Turn-Kick. Clap-Turn-Kick.

He and the Dance Lady are perfectly synchronized.

"Cassie," I say in a whisper, right into her ear so she can hear me, "who's that?"

"Who?"

"That guy out there, with the Dance Lady."

"Not sure." She blinks a few times and squints out at the dance floor. "I think he's on the soccer team with Tyler. Eighth grader."

The beat is strong and loud. I watch him dance, his sleeves cuffed up, a rope bracelet circling his wrist, one shirttail coming untucked from his khaki pants.

"Shira?"

I jump. It's Paul.

"Want to dance?"

I try to clear my mind and focus on Paul. I try to find an answer. *No, Jason's right, I'll look stupid.* Or, *No, sorry, I don't dance.* But hammering from inside is the truth: *Of course I want to dance.* I want to dance like I do up in my room, when nobody's watching. Where I twirl and spin and feel the beat of the music and the soft carpet under my feet. I want to be fashionable and graceful and full of self-confidence. I want to have beautiful hair that floats gracefully down my back, instead of a tangly mess of poodle hair. I want to be cool and smooth and coordinated and hold my hands over my head, bumping hips with my dozens of best friends. I want to not care what people think.

But out there, there's no soft carpet. The dance floor is hard and clattery, like the hallways at school, where everybody's watching and waiting for any little mistake. My hair is a mass of frizz, and I'm not cool or smooth, and I don't have dozens of best friends.

"Shira?" asks Paul again.

"No, thank you. I don't really dance," I say, which is partly true, but not nearly the truth.

Paul smiles, because that seems to be what Paul does, even when things don't go his way. Then he looks around and sees a trio of girls sitting at a table nearby and goes over. The music is loud, so I can't hear exactly what he says, but it's pretty clear what they say back, and that's "No." Then the three of them head for the dance floor, without him.

Paul walks away and comes back with two plates of chocolate strawberries. He plunks them down in the middle of our table and sits down looking content, like rejection is just a part of his everyday life.

We all reach for the strawberries, and I manage a little smile at Cassie as we both bite in, trying and failing to catch the drip of strawberry juice before it runs down our chins.

The four of us make a perfect target for the wandering fortune-teller. I see her coming with her crystal ball and a lacy veil covering most of her face. She comes up behind Jason and sneakily leans over his left shoulder.

"Aagh!" Jason cries.

"I am sensing some turmoil at this table," she says, looking into her ball. Honestly, it seems like more of a snowglobe than an official crystal ball to me. "I sense some confusion and inner turbulence . . . and yet, great hopes and dreams."

"No kidding," mutters Cassie, and Jason muffles a laugh. The lady rubs the ball and looks deeper into it.

"And, I see romance. For someone here, I see romance." That seems to be Jason's cue to return his attention to his French fries. Cassie rolls her eyes and finishes off her slushie with a very unladylike slurp. Paul seems to be focused on a stain that has magically appeared on his tie, and I force myself not to look at that boy on the dance floor.

The romance thing clearly isn't going over very well, so our fortune-teller rubs again. "I'm seeing a chance," she says, "to do something special. To be someone special. I see hard work, and accomplishment, and friendship. If you're willing to take a risk."

I know it's ridiculous. She's not a real fortune-teller.

The others have tuned out, but I look up.

And maybe it's my imagination, or all the heavy makeup she's wearing, or the purple beams reflecting off the disco ball, but I could swear that the fortune-teller meets my glance and winks at me with one dark, knowing eye.

Chapter 8

Ta-Da!

It's Monday, and I'm going to the first rehearsal.

If it doesn't work out, I can always 1) Develop a sudden, unexplained case of laryngitis that will last for another two months, 2) Ignore my fear of fast-moving hard rubber balls and join the girls' lacrosse team, or 3) Claim that I have incapacitating stage fright—which is probably the truth, anyway.

I enter the music room with my eyes down, but as soon as I look up, there's Mr. Hoover. His face breaks into a big smile. My face probably looks like I'm headed to my dentist, who still gives me bubblegum toothpaste, like mint isn't even an option.

Cassie's waving for me to sit with her, so I plop down, and a second later, Paul sits next to me.

"I can't wait to get started," Paul says, like nobody's told him that elation is not cool in seventh grade. Meanwhile, Mr. Hoover starts passing out stapled packets that say "Master Schedule."

Monica Manley is in the back row with her posse, which includes her best friend, Melinda Croce, and that tall girl Delilah.

There's a lot of talking and bouncing in chairs and boys shoving each other around, but finally Mr. Hoover plays two chords on the piano. Everybody stops talking, except for Monica and Melinda, who keep chirping and giggling.

"Okay, everybody!" he says in his most Mr. Hoover–ish upbeat way. "I know everybody's excited. But let's get started. Girls?" he says to the back row. Finally, Monica stops talking, so Melinda does, too. They fold their arms and look toward Mr. Hoover. Monica's right eyebrow is raised just a little, giving a so-whatcha-got-I-bet-it's-not-very-good look.

"We have ten weeks to put this production together," says Mr. Hoover, "and there's a lot to do. The schedule is in your hand"—he points—"AND on the board, AND in your email in-box. So, no excuses for not being where you're supposed to be. Starting tomorrow, you're each going to have your score and script with you. At *every* rehearsal." He claps his hands and rubs them together like he's getting ready to dig into a chicken parmigiana hero. "Now let me tell you about *The Music Man.*"

That seems to be the cue to a bunch of kids to start fishing through their backpacks for snacks and stretching out into sleeping positions.

"*The Music Man* takes place in a small Iowa town in Nineteen-twelve . . ."

"Nineteen-twelve?" I hear a kid behind me groan.

"The main characters are a traveling salesman and a librarian. The traveling salesman is Professor Harold Hill." Mr. Hoover holds out an open hand in a "ta-da" kind of way in Paul's direction. A couple of kids give a clap or two, and before I realize that's what I'm supposed to do, too, Mr. Hoover goes on. "So, Harold Hill comes to River City, Iowa, promising a boys' band that will save their youth from the evils of the new pool hall."

By now, kids are elbowing and kicking each other, and someone is passing around a bag of Cheetos. Mr. Hoover talks a little louder.

"He plans to take the band money and run, but it all backfires when he falls in love with"— he does another "ta-da" move toward Monica—"Marian the Librarian." Now all the girls around Monica jump in their seats and clap like Beyoncé has just entered the building. Monica raises her chin just a little and shows every one of her perfectly white teeth.

"Now, Marian is also the town music teacher, and she's helping her mother to raise her little brother, Winthrop." He doesn't "ta-da" Winthrop. Good thing, since we'd be here all day.

By the second half of Mr. Hoover's synopsis, he's lost most kids, but I hang in there to hear how the River City ladies are big gossips, and they think Marian is a snob because she reads a lot and keeps to herself. Then Harold Hill comes along, and he brings out all the great stuff in Marian that she's been too shy to show, and he ends up falling in love with her. There's another love story between a boy named Tommy and the mayor's daughter, Zaneeta. Amaryllis is a girl who likes Winthrop, and Marcellus Washburn is an old friend of Harold's who likes a lady named Ethel Toffelmeyer. Where these names came from, I'll never know.

Finally, Mr. Hoover says there are four school-board members who sing all the time—the barbershop quartet. I'm a little relieved that they don't seem to be a big part of things.

It seems like he's just about finished, but Melinda raises her hand. "Um—" She looks at Monica, who whispers something in her ear. "Are you the director?"

"I'm glad you asked, Melinda," answers Mr. Hoover, though I can't say he looks all that glad. "I'm the vocal and musical director. Ms. Germano will be our choreographer." A few kids give a clap for Ms. Germano, our guidance counselor. "Ms. Pappalardo is our acting coach." A few claps for Ms. Pappalardo, our health teacher. "And Dr. Leeds will be our lighting director." There's no applause for Dr. Leeds. It feels weird to clap for the school psychologist.

"As for our director, I'm pleased to say that our parents'

arts group has generously funded a professional artist to direct the show. Unfortunately, she can't be with us right away, but we'll anxiously await her arrival."

Monica, Melinda, and Delilah are dancing a little in their seats. I get the feeling they knew something about this already.

"Okay!" Mr. Hoover slaps his hands on his thighs. "Everybody, take out your scripts. Read your character's lines, and I'll play the cast recording of the songs as we get to them. We should have time to cover most of act one. Okay? Here we go!"

The show opens with some salesmen on a train. The eighth grader who plays the conductor tries to put a little spirit into it when he calls out "River City!" but the kid playing the anvil salesman doesn't seem to muster much enthusiasm. Mr. Hoover starts the first song. It's those salesmen, talking about cash and merchandise, fancy goods and flypaper.

"Who wrote this musical, anyway?" the kid behind me mutters. "Some guy from Home Depot?"

But the salesmen aren't just talking. They're talking in rhythm. At first the words chug with effort, like a train leaving the station, but then they gather speed as these guys argue about the oddest things, like packaged biscuits and Model T Fords. It's almost like somebody took a rap song and threw it back about a century. The words fly by, picking up speed: territory, pickle barrels, sugar barrels, and something called a hogshead. None of it makes a lot of sense, but kids are bouncing along in their seats anyway. It's hard not to. It seems like we've boarded this train made of words and rhythm and there's no chance of getting off.

After a while, they mention a salesman, Professor Harold Hill. It seems like they don't like him very much. They go on about him for a while, the pace clipping along, and then, at last, it all starts to slow down. The beat and the words get heavy, stretched out and tired, like the train is coming into the station. And when it stops, it feels like it's taken all of us right to River City.

The townspeople sing next, about Iowa, and how stubborn everyone is. And after that, Harold Hill gets everybody all worked up about the dangers of a new pool table. I can't believe how calm Paul is. He just mouths the words of "Ya Got Trouble" along with the recording like it's nothing at all. And if those salesmen were reeling off a thousand words a minute, Harold is doing a million.

"Goodnight, My Someone" puts me back in my room where it's safe and familiar, but that feeling only lasts until I see Jacey Squires' first line coming up. Paul must hear my heart pounding, or maybe he sees my script shaking in my hand, because just before it's my turn, he gives me a soft nudge with his elbow. Even though I practically whisper it, I manage to read my line.

"Seventy-Six Trombones" is the show's most famous song, and it has most of us nodding and bobbing along. Paul seems to know every word.

And then, finally, the barbershop quartet sings their first song. There's no accompaniment, just their voices, so creamy and smooth I can hardly believe they're four separate people. I focus on the first tenor singing the harmony way up high, and I think, *That's Jacey Squires. That's me.*

Then come the River City Ladies, Harold, Marian, and Marcellus, and finally, the last song in Act I, "The Wells Fargo Wagon." It's upbeat and bouncy, and Mr. Hoover gets us all singing along.

Well, almost all of us. Right in the middle, Monica squeezes her way out of her row, slinking toward the door, ducking her head, as if that's going to make her invisible. Mr. Hoover shoots a questioning look at the doorway, where Monica's mom is waiting. She flashes a stiff smile, then she takes Monica and they hurry off.

When we finish "The Wells Fargo Wagon," Mr. Hoover has us sing a melody called "The Minuet in G." He explains that Harold Hill uses this melody for something called "The Think System," telling everybody that if they sing it enough, they'll be able to play it on their instruments. Of course, that's not true, but he'll be on the train to the next town by the time they find out.

Mr. Hoover leads us through the Minuet, waving his

arms like he's conducting a full orchestra. "La-de-da-de-da-de-da-de-da," everybody sings. Even the kid sitting behind me, and the girls in the last row, and the boys who joke around. Even me.

"Great start!" Mr. Hoover calls out, and I'm about to tell Cassie that I don't think I'll get laryngitis after all, or join the lacrosse team, when I hear Mr. Hoover call my name. "Shira! Can you stay a minute?"

"Again?" whispers Cassie, just as I'm thinking exactly that.

Cassie's mom will be waiting for her, so I say, "Go on. I'll call you." Cassie holds up her hand in a phone position and nods.

Then, when everybody's finished pushing and shoving and whistling their way out of the music room, I find myself sitting in that chorus chair again, opposite Mr. Hoover.

"So," he asks. "Did you like it? The rehearsal?"

I nod.

"I knew you would," he says. "It's a great show, right?"

I nod, wondering why I'm here. Again.

"So, I'll get to the point. Something's come up."

I feel a jolt of worry. What if there *has* been a mistake? What if I'm not going to play Jacey Squires after all?

"You probably noticed that Monica had to leave early today." I nod a third time. "Well, that's the thing. She's a very talented girl, and she has lots of experience. She'll be a very good Marian. But she's going to have to miss some rehearsals. She has some auditions."

"In The City," I add. I don't know why.

"Um, yes." Mr. Hoover scratches his left temple, like he's thinking this through all over again. "So it would be great if she had an understudy. Someone to learn the part alongside her and stand in when she can't make a rehearsal." Mr. Hoover folds his arms and smiles. "And Shira, I think it would be a great opportunity for you!"

"Me?" is all I can think of saying.

"Yes! You could learn the role, and shadow Monica when your barbershop quartet rehearsals don't conflict. Marian is such a rich character. If you listen to her songs at home—"

"Oh, I have. I—" It's out of my mouth before I can stop it.

Mr. Hoover's face lights up. "Then you know! It's such a wonderful role. The more I think about it, Shira, the more I know this is a great chance for you . . ."

I listen and nod as Mr. Hoover keeps talking, about the rehearsal schedule, how I'd be helping the show, and it would be such good experience for me. But all I can think is, Jacey Squires is one thing. Marian the Librarian is another. Hearing the barbershop quartet, all four voices leaning on each other, combining with each other—I can do that. But Marian, just Marian. That's different.

I tell Mr. Hoover I have to get home. I'll think it over. I promise. Then I hurry out of the music room and start on my way home, thinking about Monica. I mean Marian. No, I mean Monica.

Our paths have crossed once before.

Chapter 9

Starfish

I was in fourth grade, Monica was in fifth.
We were put in the same swim group in camp—Starfish.
Swimming was the one place where grades were mixed. I
didn't know Monica, but I'd heard her say that her parents
had "parked her there" for a week, because she was going to
sleepaway and then to Nantucket with her mother for the
rest of the summer.

We were sitting around in a circle, waiting for our turn
to swim. We fourth graders sat cross-legged, but the fifth
graders had their legs stretched out straight into the middle
of the circle. One of Monica's braceleted ankles lay crossed
over the other. She wiggled her toes, which were polished in
a pink-orange color that reminded me of cantaloupe. The
girls leaned back on their arms, bending and unbending
their knees, pointing their toes.

"I ran out of gel, so I used my dad's shaving cream," one
of them said.

"Gross," said the other, "you *shave* your legs? I use Nair.
Feel, they're like the softest soft."

"It gave me a rash," said the other girl.

"You know Amber uses her mother's electric razor?" said a girl with the longest toes I'd ever seen. They looked like they had three separate joints. "Is that so totally gross?" They traded gross-out sounds, and then Monica held up her hands, showing her matching pink-orange nails, and leaned into the circle like she was going to reveal a secret. She ran a finger down her beautifully tan calf.

"Wax," was all she said. The others nodded silently.

I was still sitting cross-legged, squeezing my unshaven calves so tight together that I'd probably need about two days to shake out the pins and needles. I prayed that we'd be called to the pool, but our counselor was busy talking to a super tan lifeguard with a heart tattoo on his bicep. Then I saw Monica look at me and the other fourth graders, our legs twisted in pretzels, and I knew we were out of time.

"Hey. Let's see everybody's," she said in a fun-loving voice. "Come on, everyone put your legs in the middle." We didn't move, but then Monica turned drill sergeant and snapped, "Everyone!" so I slowly unfurled my legs, and the others did, too, putting our feet into the middle, revealing our unshaved, un-Naired, un-waxed legs. I could see Monica and her friends holding it in, just long enough so that they could follow Monica's lead and burst into laughs, pointing and giggling. The group next to us looked over to see what was happening.

I felt my eyes fill with tears, and of course my face turning raspberry, but finally our counselor came to the rescue, calling us over to the pool and giving us our instructions to swim to the end and back.

As it happened, Starfish got broken up into Flounders and Sole after they saw us swim, so I didn't see Monica again. I don't know if she remembers that day, but I do. I know adults tell you that one day you'll look back and laugh. I don't know if that's true. You don't get over that kind of fourth-grade stuff easily. Maybe it's gone by the time you're seventy-five, but it stays with you for a long time. At least through seventh grade.

When I get home, Sophie is in the kitchen.

"Where's Mom?" I ask.

"She's finishing some work," says Sophie. "What do you want to tell her? Anything you say to her you can say to me."

I plop my backpack down. "I'll wait."

Sophie sits and stares at me. "Is it about the show?"

"None of your business."

"My friends voted seventeen to five that you should do it."

"Do what?"

"The boy's part in the play."

"Seventeen to five? You have twenty-two friends?"

"Well, recess friends."

"Don't you have anything better to do at recess? Box ball or something?"

"No. Three girls even said they'd like to wear a mustache. And a boy said he'd be into wearing a dress. You're breaking gender norms. Everyone thinks it's cool."

"It's not about the mustache, Sophie," I say with a sigh.

Mom comes in and sits down, rubbing her neck like she always does when she's been working hard. She's an editor, so she's always correcting other people's mistakes.

"Shira has something to tell you," says Sophie.

I take a deep breath. "Mr. Hoover wants me to understudy Marian."

Mom sits back in her chair and stares at me. "But that's the lead." She turns to look at my sister. "Sophie didn't tell me that."

"Maybe Sophie doesn't hear everything." I look at Sophie, who seems disappointed in herself. Of course, this is all new territory. My life hasn't exactly offered a lot worth gossiping about.

"I'd just be a stand-in," I say. "When Monica has an audition or something."

"Well, you know," says Mom. "I bet that girl could learn a few things from you."

"I doubt it," I say.

"And sometimes understudies get called in to save the day."

"So are you gonna do it?" Sophie asks.

"I don't know."

"What does Cassie think?" Sophie doesn't give up.

"How do you know I asked Cassie?"

"Well, didn't you?"

I sigh again. I texted her as soon as I left the music room. "Yes. She wants me to. But I don't know. First it was Jacey Squires. Now it's this big role."

"And Monica Manley," adds Sophie.

"Well, Mr. Hoover must think you're pretty special," says Mom. "And I know you are. But you're the one who has to believe it."

It's such a motherish thing to say.

I pick up my stuff and go upstairs. I hear Sophie following behind me. "You should do it," she says, "but watch out for Monica Manley. She's dangerous."

"Dangerous?"

"Creatures in the wild react badly when their territory is threatened."

"I'm not a threat. I'm just a lowly seventh grader. And it's middle school, Sophie. Not National Geographic."

"Same thing," she says, and I have to admit, for a fourth grader, Sophie has an impressive and troubling grasp of middle school life.

Chapter 10

Sincere

There are four of us in the music room the next day. It's our first barbershop quartet rehearsal. I can't believe that playing Jacey Squires now seems like the easy decision. We have forty-five minutes with Mr. Hoover, and then we'll go join the "Ya Got Trouble" rehearsal in the auditorium.

I know Jason from the Bar Mitzvah, and the other barbershop members are Felix and Vijay. I remember Vijay from a math class and Felix from English last year, but I've never spoken a word to either of them. Vijay has dark hair that flops over one eye and that sprouty look like he's outgrowing his clothes overnight. Felix is skinny with reddish hair. His face is pale, and it somehow seems like he should have a bunch of freckles to finish the picture, but he doesn't. He sits in a slight ducking position, like he's afraid that something's going to come flying at him any second.

"Okay," Mr. Hoover finally says. "Let's get you guys started!"

Us guys. If my eyebrow could raise like Monica's did, it would. But it can't, so it doesn't.

"I love the barbershop quartet," says Mr. Hoover. "You're members of the River City school board, and you've hated each other for years." I send a nervous smile Felix's way, and he quickly looks down at the ground. "The mayor is suspicious of Harold Hill, and he asks you to get Hill's credentials—his sales license, proof that he's legit. But every time you get near him, he distracts you by getting you to sing. And every time you sing, you become inseparable, a harmonious unit, best buddies. It's all about the power of music," he explains, "how it can transform people."

I look around at our ragtag group. We're going to need a pretty fair amount of transformation.

Mr. Hoover sits down at the piano. "But you'll see. Let's try 'Goodnight, Ladies.'"

Mr. Hoover plays each line separately, going over our parts one by one.

Vijay starts at second tenor. I can understand why Mr. Hoover picked him as the melody guy. He has a really nice, smooth voice and he sings like he sits in the chair—long legs stretched out, loose and comfortable. Felix is next. He nods his head with every note, his voice cracks every now and then, and his forehead wrinkles up overtime as he sings. But he gets through his line pretty well and then collapses back in his chair in relief.

Jason booms out the low notes, but unfortunately, the more he sings, the more he sweats. It's just one song, and he looks like he's just come back from a trek through the Sahara.

Then everyone looks at me. It's my turn. Of course, my heart is beating like a snare drum.

But Mr. Hoover is looking at me the same way he did in the audition, with so much encouragement, so I start.

I'm surprised, hearing my own voice, like it's a part of me, but separate. Once it leaves me, it's almost like a ball I've thrown. It sails away, on its own.

When I'm done, we try putting it together. That's when things don't go so well.

Jason loses his way completely, and then Felix slips into singing the melody line with Vijay, and then it all collapses like one of those people pyramids, when everyone tumbles to the floor, with me on the top. Jason lets out a disgusted groan and Vijay break into giggles. Felix looks at his music like the notes are going to jump off the page and bite him.

But Mr. Hoover convinces us that it always starts out this way. We try the second verse, which seems to go a little better, and then Mr. Hoover jumps right into the next song.

"So," he says, "'Sincere,' starts with 'Ice Cream.'" Jason's face lights up, but Mr. Hoover is just talking about the first line of the song. "Harold Hill gets them singing by showing them that it's just talking, but really slow. He starts with Olin. That's you, Jason."

Mr. Hoover plays Jason's note, and he sings it in a deep voice, "Ice creeeeeeeeeem."

"Now, hold that, Jason. Take a little breath if you have to, and come back in." Then he plays Felix's note, which is a little higher, "Ice creeeeeeeem." Felix holds that note, and Mr. Hoover adds Vijay's. And then way up on top, I sing a really high "Ice creeeeeeem." We each hold our note, and look at each other with amazement, because all of a sudden there's this thing happening. This beautiful, ringing harmony.

"Now," says Mr. Hoover, "That's the warm-up. Once they hear how good they sound, the four of them break into song." Mr. Hoover plays each of our parts, and he sings Harold Hill's line:

How can there be . . .

And then we come in.

. . . any sin in "sincere"
Where is the good in "goodbye"?
Your apprehensions confuse me dear
Puzzle and mystify.

It actually doesn't sound half bad. We go on, slowly.

Tell me, what can be fair in "farewell," dear,
While one single star shines above?
How can there be any sin in "sincere"?
Aren't we sincerely in love?

"Are the other songs so lovey-dovey?" asks Felix, looking like his aunt just planted a wet one on his cheek.

"What do you mean?" says Vijay. "Why is there sin in 'sincere'? Where's the good in 'goodbye'? It's wordplay. I love wordplay."

Mr. Hoover looks delighted by all of this. "Before you know it, you'll be a unit, arms around each other, a true barbershop quartet."

Watching the stains spread on Jason's T-shirt, I'm reminded what a terrible plan that arms-around-shoulders idea is.

We go over another song called "It's You," and then we rehearse the spoken parts, which consist of bickering about the weather and if the trains are running on time and before we know it, our forty-five minutes are up.

"Okay!" says Mr. Hoover. This rehearsal seems to have kicked his happiness up a notch. "Vijay, Jason, and Felix, you go join the rehearsal in the auditorium. Shira, how about if we pop into room five. Monica is finishing up in there and you can chat—about the understudy thing."

I take a deep breath and nod.

"I've asked Shira to be Monica's understudy," says Mr. Hoover. "And I'm hoping she'll say yes."

As I follow Mr. Hoover to the door, I hear Vijay's voice. "Have fun."

And then Jason's. "May the baton be with you."

Chapter 11

Skin Deep

As we approach room 5, two girls and a boy are just leaving. I recognize Sean Battaglia. He's playing Winthrop.

"Is Monica still inside?" asks Mr. Hoover.

"Um, yeah," says Sean. "She's counting her lines."

I figure that must be some theatrical term.

"Okay," says Mr. Hoover, but he looks a little confused.

Inside, Monica is sitting with her script in her lap. Ms. Pappalardo is on the far side of the room, texting.

"So," says Mr. Hoover. "How did it go?"

Ms. Pappalardo looks up. "Oh! Fine! We read through the whole porch scene." Her phone chimes and she looks at the screen. "Poor Kyle. My littlest one is home with strep."

For a health teacher, Ms. Pappalardo's kids are sick a lot.

"Well, Monica and Shira are going to spend a few minutes getting to know each other. Right, Monica?" Monica is staring at her script. I think I see one shoulder rise about a centimeter and fall again. Ms. Pappalardo nods, but her attention is back on her phone. Mr. Hoover rubs his palms together and bounces on his toes. "Okay!" he says. "Have fun, you two."

As he turns to go, I want to grab him by his tweedy gray lapels and shout, "Please don't leave me!" But he just gives a thumbs-up, and the door closes behind him.

"Hi," I say, but Monica doesn't answer. She's looking at the script. Her finger trails slowly down the page, her lips moving slightly.

I stand there, waiting for her to finish ignoring me. Her hair shines with a frosty sheen under the flourescent classroom lights. It makes me think of that ribbon candy they sell around Christmas that shatters all over the floor if you drop it. Her legs are neatly crossed, with one shoe dangling from a bouncing toe.

After about two minutes, she looks up and says, "Sixty-five."

"Huh?" I say.

"I have sixty-five lines in the first act."

"Wow," I reply.

"My acting coach, Ms. Felt, says that each line is a pearl. You string them together to make a beautiful necklace."

"Wow," I say again. "A pearl. That's kind of nice."

"Well, yeah. But if you don't get enough pearls, it's hardly going to be worth it. A bit part, you get maybe just a couple of pearls, you're not even going to have enough to make a choker." She flips to Act II and starts to count again.

"You don't think she meant it like even one line can be . . . important? Like, a gem?"

Monica's finger stops moving and she looks up.

"No," she says. Then she shakes her head like somebody has put some strange, unpleasant thought in it. "No. That's not what she meant." She goes back to counting.

"So, have you memorized some of your lines already?" I ask.

"Memorized?" Monica sighs and looks up at me with pity in her eyes. "There's so much more to it than *memorizing*. Ms. Felt calls it learning the role 'by heart.'" She glances back down at the script, then back up at me. "I mean, an *under*study can just memorize. But *my* job is to learn it '*by heart.*'" She makes a fist and clutches it to her collarbone, nowhere near her heart, really. "I audition for commercials in The City, you know."

"I've heard," I say.

"Well, that's no different. By *heart*." She pounds her collarbone again.

"Have you started learning the songs?" I ask.

"One of them. It's pretty lame. What's it called?" She digs into a black messenger bag that's overflowing with scarves, a makeup kit, and what I think is an extra pair of shoes. She comes up with her score, which must have been stuffed in there all curled up over the weekend. "Here. 'Goodnight,

My Someone.'" I'm about to tell her how I listened to it, too, when she says, "It's about losers."

"Losers?"

"She's saying there's got to be somebody out there, because the guys she knows are just way pathetic."

"I don't know, Monica. I thought she was just saying—"

"I mean, Marian's pretty much a bore. A librarian and a music teacher? Please."

I want to tell her she's wrong. Marian is not a bore at all. She's just a little shy, and lonely.

But Monica powers ahead. "It's no surprise she can't find anybody to date." Then she stops and sighs. "I can totally get into her motivation, though. I mean, look at the losers in this school. Drew is like the only decent guy here."

"Drew?" I ask.

"Drew Jensen." She looks me over like she's deciding if I'm worthy of any kind of "stay away from him" type warning. I'm obviously not. "He's on stage crew. He's going to be building my sets." Then she looks up at the corner of the room, like she's addressing some god of theater. "If life was fair, he'd be my leading man."

I think about Paul, how excited he is to be playing Harold Hill. "You don't think Paul will be good?"

She lets out a puff of air and says, "He's shorter than I am." Like that explains everything.

"He must be pretty talented if he got the part."

"Please," she says, tucking a stray lock of hair behind her ear. "I mean, let's face it, talent is only skin deep."

As I try to unscramble that, she goes on. "And listen. While we're on the subject, a few ground rules? Just because you're in a show with someone doesn't mean you hang out with them."

"Oh . . . don't worry, Monica," I say quickly. "I don't expect you to hang out with me or anything."

"Me?" she says, looking horrified. "Hang out with you? No, *that's* not happening."

She brushes some imaginary speck off her jeans. "I was talking about you and Paul."

"Me and Paul?"

Monica sighs. "Tyler's Bar Mitzvah?" She nods. "Word travels. Don't let him think he's your new BFF."

I guess I look lost, because Monica says, "Look. I don't know why I'm bothering, but I can't help it. Generosity is in my nature. Stand up. I'll show you how to shake a geek."

I'm trying to process what she's offering. A glimpse behind the curtain. A clue to the power of girls like her. But then I think about Paul. He's not a geek. I don't need to shake him. So I say, "No, Monica, I—"

But then she says "Stand up" again, and I'm suddenly back in fourth grade, and there's no saying no to Monica. I stand up.

"Act one, scene seven," says Monica, for Ms. Pappalardo's

benefit. Then she says to me, "Okay, you be Paul and I'll be you. Walk up behind me and say something."

My mind is a blank, but finally I come up with, "Hello, Shira. I had fun at the Bar Mitzvah—"

"Oh, please. Even he's not that lame. Try again." She strikes her pose and I try again.

"Hey, Shira. How's it going?"

I know she hears me. I'm right next to her. But she doesn't react. It's like I'm not even here.

"Monica?" I say.

She looks at her fingers and picks at the amoeba-like splotch of polish on her left fingernail and turns her head just slightly, like she's heard a distant sound. Then she looks at her watch and walks away like I'm invisible.

"See?" she says, turning around and smiling.

"But I couldn't do that."

"Why not?"

"Because . . . you're acting like he's not even there. How would you feel if somebody did that to you?"

"Oh, they did. But they don't anymore."

"But didn't you feel bad when they did?"

"Yeah. So?" She sits back down and picks up her script again.

She looks at me, and then at the door, and then back at her script. She starts counting again and I get the message. She knows how to shake a geek.

Chapter 12

Goal

Out in the hallway I can hear that the townspeople rehearsal is wrapping up. Ms. Germano calls out a last reminder: "Front row does the kicks. Back row, *no kicking*."

I could wait for Cassie, but my mind is on overload, buzzing from the rehearsal, the singing, Monica.

My shortcut home is across the playing field. I let the heavy side door swing shut behind me. It's warm today. Autumn still hasn't quite made its appearance. I'm about to start across the field, but the boys soccer team is out there doing some drills, so I walk around the perimeter.

I try not to watch. It's not great to be caught staring at boys. But I look around, and nobody's watching me watching them, so I do. They line up, their backs to me, trotting sideways, one foot crossing in front of the other, then side-stepping, crossing, and side-stepping again.

I see Tyler Glass and a few of his buddies on one end of the line. Then further down, the boys get a little bigger, their steps a little more confident. Eighth graders. There's a kind of goofy grace in the exercise. They're like a ragged chorus line, except instead of music, there's just the sound of shin guards slapping against their legs.

Then, just like at the Bar Mitzvah, my eyes lock on one boy who looks different. I recognize his light brown hair and the smoothness in his motions. More dancelike. It's in the relaxed way his arms move, and his hands. His steps are even, not all jerky like the others.

Someone calls out an order and they break up the chorus line. They start bouncing balls on their knees, off their heads, into the goal. A part of me wants to stay and stare, but some of the boys face my way, so I pull my glance away and set my sights on the far corner of the field.

Then there's a *BOOM*. I turn around to see a ball sailing toward me. I automatically wince and duck, but it flies way over my head. It lands about ten yards in front of me and bounces off the fence.

I don't know what to do. If I pick it up, I'll have to throw it back, or kick it, or walk it in to the boys on the field.

Someone will come get it, I think. I don't have to get involved.

But then I hear, "Hey!"

I turn to look, and it's that boy.

"Hey, toss it here," he says to me, with a wave.

Clearly, pretending I don't hear is not an option. The ball is right at my feet, so I pick it up. But I can't move.

The boy holds his hands out in a questioning motion, then shrugs at my uselessness and starts to jog over.

All I can think of is the way I felt when I was four years old and got separated from my parents at the circus. A clown picked me up and asked who I belonged to, and I froze then like I'm frozen now. Except this boy is not a clown. Not even close.

He's standing opposite me, close, breathing hard. I can practically feel the heat coming from him. The exercise or the warm air has made red splotches come out on his cheeks, and there's a thin layer of sweat on his forehead. I try to keep my breathing steady, try not to look at his face, not to stare at his arms, or his hands, now resting so casually on his hips.

Someone calls out, "Drew!"

"I'm getting it!" he calls, and then he turns back and reaches for the ball. I think my knees might buckle and I'll go down right there. "Hey," he says to me, pointing to the soccer ball. "Can I . . . have that?"

I somehow manage to reach out and hand it over.

He says "Thanks" and gives me a half smile, which is more than I deserve, having made him come all the way over here and practically beg for the stupid ball.

I watch as he drops the soccer ball and gives it a few little nudges. He sends it up in the air with a jab of his toe, giving it spin, and it circles happily back to him. Then he gives it a strong, hard kick that sends it flying in a magnificent arc, and he jogs back toward the others.

I follow the flight of the ball and see it heading for the goal.

And I'm not the only one watching. On the other side of the field, standing in the school's side doorway, I see Monica, looking down, arms folded, her hair lightly blowing in the breeze. Only she doesn't see that the ball lands smack dab in the center of the goal. Because even from a distance I can tell that her eyes are narrowed and laser-like, and focused. On me.

When I get home, I go up to my room, where Sophie is waiting, sitting on my bed. "So, are you understudying?" she asks.

"Go away," I answer.

"You have to," says Sophie, giving a little push off and bouncing back on the bed, "or my rep is ruined."

"Your rep?"

"Yes. I told everyone that you're understudying Maria."

"Marian."

"Marian. And if you quit, then my rep will be ruined."

"And what? You won't be popular?"

Sophie shakes her head. "You're really in the dark ages, aren't you? My grade is post-popular. Bullying is so done."

"Well, that's good news."

"Yeah," she says, scrunching up her face. "There's still Compost Club, though."

"Compost Club? Are you in it?"

"No way. Those kids are untouchable." Sophie looks like she's even puzzled herself, but she snaps out of it. "Anyway, it's not just about me. My rep is tied to yours."

"I don't have a rep."

"Of course you do. You just don't take care of it."

"Please leave my room," I say, and point to the door. Sophie gets up, but she hovers in the doorway.

"Listen," she says. "You can't back out now. We'd both suffer. And Mom and Dad would be so sad. Think of them, if you don't care about me."

I give Sophie a little push and close my door.

I take her place on my bed. I try to focus on the decision I have to make, but my mind keeps going back to the soccer field. I picture Drew reaching out for the ball. Waiting patiently. How he said, "Can I . . . have that?" Not an especially memorable sentence. Except that he said it to me.

"So?" It's Sophie. She's still outside my door.

"Leave me alone," I call.

"Do the right thing," she says.

I think about my time with Monica. I know what I have to do. It has nothing to do with Sophie, nothing to do with my parents. It has everything to do with Marian. She's not boring and she's not a snob and "Goodnight, My Someone" is not about losers. In a strange way, I feel like I want to get to know Marian better. And protect her from Monica.

I pick up the score and turn to Marian's first song. "Piano Lesson." I look at "Will I Ever Tell You?" and "My White Knight" and "Till There Was You." And I know if I'm going to understand Marian better, I can't put this off. I've got to get started right now.

Chapter 13

Dum Da Da-Da-Da

Mr. Hoover is thrilled when I tell him that I'll be Monica's understudy, but for the first few days, it seems like it was all a false alarm and that Monica's audition schedule won't interfere with the show after all.

Until today.

It's a rainy October day, and we've finished rehearsing "It's You" in the music room. Mr. Hoover has just left to lead the River City Ladies in one of their songs next door when Monica comes in. She plunks her score on top of the piano and looks around the room—everywhere but at us.

"Are you looking for—" starts Vijay.

"My bag. It's right there." She heads over to that huge bag of stuff, picks it up, and heads for the door just as Paul comes in. "I have to go," she tells him.

"You can't," he says. "We're doing 'Marian the Librarian.'"

"Well, you'll have to do it without me." She's unwrapping a piece of gum and popping it in her mouth. "I have an audition. And anyway, that's your song."

"No, it's not. You're in it, too."

"Do I sing in it?"

"No, but we do the song together. We have to work out the choreography with Ms. Germano. You react to what I'm singing. The song is *called* 'Marian the Librarian.'"

She stops to think, like maybe that does make a difference, but then she shakes her head. "Still, not my song. I can't miss an audition to 'react.'" She makes two little squiggles in the air around "react." "Anyway, it's really just blocking, and first blocking rehearsals are boring." Then she looks at me. "Let her do it."

Then, just like she showed me, she scans the room, and as if there's nobody here at all, she leaves.

"What's blocking?" asks Jason.

"It means the staging," Paul says. "The way we move around."

"Do you think she really has an audition?" asks Felix.

Paul shrugs. "I don't know. Outside of rehearsal, she pretends not to know me, and in rehearsal she just talks about feeling her character, and somebody named Miss Felt."

"Her acting teacher," I say.

"Well, Monica has more experience than we do," says Vijay.

"Experience auditioning, maybe," says Jason. "But I haven't exactly seen her eating a Wendy's burger on TV. Have you?"

He might have a point.

"I just hope she goes over her songs with Miss Felt," says Paul. "It doesn't seem like she's even started."

Felix is over by the piano. He picks up Monica's score. "Doesn't look like she will," he says.

A few more kids are starting to wander in for the "Marian the Librarian" rehearsal. Soon Ms. Germano comes in with Mr. Hoover.

"Monica has an audition, so Shira will play Marian, okay?" Paul tells them.

Mr. Hoover shoots me a wink, and Ms. Germano says, "Excellent." Being a guidance counselor, she's pretty much happy when anybody decides to do anything.

The last of the kids have come into the music room. "Library patrons!" Ms. Germano calls out. "Everyone find a seat. We have a lot to do!"

It takes a while for everyone to settle down, something that my stomach doesn't seem to be able to manage. But Paul gives me a thumbs-up, and Ms. Germano is already getting started.

"We're in the library," she says, "and Harold Hill has come to woo Marian. He's following her around the library, singing about how much he loves her. But she keeps shushing him, because first of all, it's a library and there's no talking. And second, she's this shy small-town librarian, and he's this sharp city salesman.

So, she keeps trying to get him to stop, and he keeps following her."

"Isn't that stalking?" asks Frankie. "It sounds like stalking."

"Well," says Ms. Germano, looking a little flustered. "Maybe my description didn't convey the comic element. You see, it's a library, so really the only threat is that he'll disturb the library patrons."

"But he's following her around, and she doesn't want him to," says Frankie. "That's stalking."

"Yes, well, but you see, it's a comedy. For instance, she asks what he'd like to take out from the library—and he says, 'The librarian!'" Ms. Germano smiles. Frankie doesn't.

"I think in Iowa, at the time, it was considered witty," Ms. Germano says. "But, let's start the song, and I hope you'll see its charm."

First we map out who goes where. Ms. Germano lines up the patrons to check out their books, and she has me stamping the due date in them, like they used to do back then. Then she has me pretend to shelve books while Paul follows and gets in my way. The library patrons walk around, holding their hands up like they're reading books. We try it a few times and it isn't too scary, or too exciting, either, but that all changes when we add the music.

The piano starts the song with a clear, punchy beat.

"*Dum—da-duh-duh-duh, Dum—da-duh-duh-duh* . . ." The kids come up with their pretend books, and I pretend stamp them right on the beat—"*thunk*" on the stamp pad, then "*thunk*" on the book—until Paul comes up and sticks his hand under my stamper to get my attention. I look up, and he gives his best charming smile. And suddenly, he's Harold Hill and I'm Marian the Librarian. He starts singing over the "*Dum—da-duh-duh-duh,*" but all stretched out, like,

Ma---------rian.

Madam libra----------rian.

He holds out those "*a*"s, and it sounds kind of pleading and hypnotic and funny all at once.

Then he goes on, proclaiming his love, and I walk around the room like we practiced, but this time I'm feeling like Marian. Like someone who's never gotten any attention and suddenly there's this guy, and he's focused on me. The library patrons are walking to the beat, making a circle around the room, and I'm in the center of it. Me, Marian. Me, Shira.

"Clutch some books tight, Marian. You're a prim and proper librarian!" she instructs me. "Straight posture! Prim and proper!" The tune turns snappy and bouncy, and Paul follows me around, singing,

What can I do, my dear,

To catch your ear,

I love you madly, madly,
Madam librarian,
Marian . . .

I feel myself wanting to grin, but I keep my prim and proper posture and make my steps snappy and even toss my head once as I turn away from Harold. Finally, when we get to the last part, Paul gets down on one knee and spreads his arms out. Ms. Germano signals for everyone to stop, and he looks at me and sings,

It's a long-lost cause
I can never win,
For the civilized world accepts
as unforgivable sin
Any talking out loud
with any librarian,
Such as Marian.
Madam librarian.

She signals for the library patrons to walk to the beat of the last "Dum—da-duh-duh-duh," making their exits, and then Mr. Hoover finishes with a final chord.

By the time Paul has reached his final "Marian," all the kids who are library patrons are laughing, because the song really is pretty funny. Even Frankie is smiling.

We run it through one more time, and I realize I'm not nervous at all. In fact, I'm feeling like I could do it again and again and again. I'm not really me, but I'm not pretending, either. It's some free space in between.

And I figure out something about Marian, too. She doesn't want to be bothered, but she also does want to be bothered. Because under the pushy salesman exterior, Harold's really a good guy. He's clever and charming, and nothing exciting like this ever happens in River City, Iowa. Marian's starting to see that Harold has another side to him. And she's starting to think that maybe she does, too. Maybe all it takes is for someone to push past her defenses, to see what's hiding underneath.

Chapter 14

Ding Dong Ding

A few days later, we're in the music room, waiting for Mr. Hoover to start rehearsal. Vijay, Felix, and Jason start up a conversation about our social studies assignment. The two social studies teachers have been at Hedgebrook for ages, and they've been giving this assignment every year since forever. We have to research farming in the Massachusetts Bay Colony in 1650, choose crops, and pick two animals for our family farm. It's due Friday, but I've managed to mostly ignore it for the past week.

"My crops are corn, beans, and squash," says Vijay.

"Corn, beans, and peas," says Felix.

Jason shakes his head slowly. "They must've gotten really sick of corn and beans. How about livestock?"

"Chickens and dairy cows," says Felix. "I'd have eggs, milk, and cheese for life. Do you think that's right?"

"There's no right or wrong answer, Felix," says Vijay. "As long as they had them in 1650 New England."

"But do you think she wants us to pick something different?"

"I think she wants us to think for ourselves."

"Oh, come *on*." Felix stares at Vijay. "When did a teacher ever really want us to think for ourselves?"

Vijay shrugs and turns to Jason, "You've got cows and sheep, right, Jason?"

"Yup. Beef, milk, and sweaters," replies Jason. "I really like sweaters."

"This is a dumb assignment. It's all hypothetical," says Felix. "It's like, you're stranded on a desert island, what movie would you watch? Like there's some magical power source? We're never going to own a farm in 1650 Massachusetts, so what's the point?"

"The point is, you're taken out of your comfort zone," says Vijay.

"I like my comfort zone," says Felix.

"Well, I like hypotheticals," says Vijay. "You get to see how people's minds work."

"Hey, would I need a sheepdog?" asks Jason. "For the sheep?"

"Two dogs came over on the *Mayflower*," I say, and all three of them look at me. I know I'm blushing, because even when I think I have something to say, when I hear myself say it and then people look at me, I immediately think it's a mistake.

But Vijay surprises me. "I read that, too!" he says. "And did you know that llamas make good shepherds? They're protective, and they chase away intruders."

"And when they get really irritated, they spit," I add, because I once went to a farm and they warned us about that.

"Cool," says Jason.

"Awesome," says Felix.

"But they didn't have llamas in Massachusetts in 1650," Vijay says. He seems a little disappointed, which is kind of endearing.

"Wait!" Felix sits up suddenly. "Horses! I bet it's a trick question. We forgot transportation. Did they have horses yet?"

"We have cows," says Jason. "You could ride a cow in a pinch, couldn't you?"

"Like I said," Vijay mutters, "you learn a lot about people."

I think he must have the same picture in his mind as I do—Jason bouncing along on top of a brown-and-white Elsie.

Just then, Mr. Hoover pokes his head in. "Barbershop! Get started with 'Lida Rose' and I'll be in soon. Vijay, you play piano, right?" Vijay wiggles his fingers in the air and nods. "Play each part through as many times as it takes. These are tough musical lines. Ms. Pappalardo will be here to help. I have to look in on the 'Shipoopi' rehearsal and the River City Ladies."

Ms. Pappalardo comes in as Vijay takes his place by the piano. She sits in the corner of the room and smiles.

"Okay," says Vijay, "'Lida Rose.' Let's do it.'" He plays each of our lines. Jason and Felix take out their scores and follow along. I learned my part last night, so I don't bother with my score.

We sing it through individually, then finally, when we feel ready, we put it together. Vijay plays the first line, *"Lida Rose, I'm home again, Rose,"* that Harold sings to get us started. Then he plays our four notes and we start, slowly.

To get the sun back in the sky

It's not too bad. We run a few more lines.

Lida Rose, I'm home again, Rose,
About a thousand kisses shy

Felix wrinkles up his nose. "A thousand kisses? Really?"

Ding, dong, ding,
I can hear the chapel bell chime

On "chime," we all stop and look at each other.

"Something's off," says Vijay.

"Um," I say, "Felix, that's a D-flat. You sang a D-natural."

Vijay plays it on the piano, then Felix sings the line. "Yeah," he says, giving me an odd look. "You're right. I've got it now."

We go on to one of my favorite lines, *"At the least suggestion I'll pop the question,"* and then,

Lida Rose, I'm home again, Rose,
without a sweetheart to my name,
Lida Rose, now everyone knows
that I am hoping you're the same.

When we get to "hoping you're the same," it sounds off again. But this time it's Jason.

"Jason," I say, "it's an E-flat." Vijay plays Jason's part on the piano and Jason sings along.

"Right again," he says, looking at me. "But how did you know the exact note I got wrong? You're not even looking at the music."

"I . . . heard it," I say. I'm not sure what he means. "We all heard it, right?" I look around, but no one is nodding.

"We heard that something was wrong. But you knew exactly which note," says Felix.

"Hey, Shira," says Vijay, "do you know what note this is?" He's covering his playing hand with his other hand, blocking the keys. I'm not sure why.

"It's a G. Don't you know it's a G?"

"And this?" he says, playing another note.

"C-sharp. Why?"

They're all looking at me, and I wish they'd stop.

"You just . . . know?" Jason is asking.

Felix points at the piano. "Without looking? You know just by hearing it?"

"Of course . . ." I say. I'm confused. If I saw a picture of a daisy, it wouldn't have to have the word "daisy" under it. A daisy is a daisy. A C-sharp is a C-sharp.

Vijay plays three notes. "What notes are these?"

"D, F-sharp, A," I say. "Why?" I don't know what's going on. Are they mad because I told them they sang wrong notes? Is there some punchline to this, because if there is, it's not a very funny joke.

Jason's mouth is open, Felix's forehead is wrinkled up like an accordion, Vijay is shaking his head, and Ms. Pappalardo has come over and she's staring, too.

"What?" I say.

"I'm getting Mr. Hoover," says Jason, then he runs out of the room like he's just seen some kid riding a cow.

Chapter 15

Perfect

"It's called perfect pitch," says Mr. Hoover.
"I thought you might have it."

I can tell that he thinks this is a good thing, but the way everybody's staring at me makes me feel like I have some kind of disease, or one of those superpowers you can't control and you end up smashing windows and blowing things up by mistake.

"Wait," I say. "I have what?"

"Perfect pitch. I'll show you. Sing an A for me."

Everybody's looking at me again, and I can feel the blush starting to climb from my neck to my cheeks to my ears. But everybody's waiting, so I sing a quick "la" on an A.

Mr. Hoover plays an A on the piano and they all look at me like I've done a triple somersault or something.

"And what are these notes?" He plays three notes, one low on the keyboard, then in the middle, then up high.

"G, B . . ." I hesitate a little, just so I don't seem like a know-it-all, but it's no use pretending I don't know. "D," I finish. "But . . . doesn't everybody . . . ?"

Mr. Hoover shakes his head.

"Felix, you can't . . ."

Felix shakes his head, his eyebrows knitting into a little upside-down V.

"We can't just pick an A out of the air like that," says Vijay. "Or name random notes."

"So," I say, trying to figure this out, "you know that that's blue . . ." I point to Mr. Hoover's light blue shirt, this time with a little sheep icon above the pocket. ". . . and that's orange . . ." I hold up my score. "But you don't know that . . ." And right on cue, Jason's phone dings a message. "You don't know that that's an A-flat?"

More headshakes.

Mr. Hoover still looks like the most cheerful person in the universe. "Most people can repeat a note," he explains. "They can sing a tune once you start them out. They learn to read music and they know what note to sing relative to another note. But with perfect pitch, you know what note it is instinctively. Like you just said, like blue is blue or orange is orange."

Or a daisy is a daisy.

Suddenly the door flies open, and Paul comes running in. I have to wonder if full speed ahead is his only gear.

"So, what's Shira's secret power?" he says, looking at me like he's ready to see me climb straight up the walls. Jason is trying to slip his phone back into his pocket, as if I'm not going to figure out that he's the one who texted Paul.

"Shira has perfect pitch," says Vijay.

"That's so cool!" says Paul. "I've read about that. So, if I play a note—"

"Yeah, we did that," says Felix.

"Or if I ask you to sing a B-flat—"

"We did that, too," says Vijay, and I see him motion to Paul with a super-speed shake of his head. I think he knows that in a minute I'm going to bolt out of here and never come back.

"It's fairly rare in general, but not uncommon among musicians," says Mr. Hoover. "Sometimes it can even make it harder to enjoy music, because you know the true pitch for a note, and if someone is flat, or sharp, it sounds worse to you than to anybody else."

Then there's a loud "Ahem." I look up. It's Monica, standing in the doorway, examining the toe of her boot while she waits for us to notice her.

"Monica," says Mr. Hoover, waving her in. "Come in. We just discovered something. Shira has perfect pitch." Monica shifts her gaze from her boot toe to me. Her expression doesn't change even the slightest bit.

Mr. Hoover's phone buzzes in his pocket and he looks at the screen. "Oh boy. Seems like Zaneeta Shinn and Tommy Djilas are having some problems."

"Zaneeta is Melinda's part," says Jason. Monica shoots him a squinty-eyed look. "What? I'm just saying."

"I better get over there," says Mr. Hoover. Mr. Hoover's phone buzzes again and he looks at the screen. "Whoo boy." And he hurries out.

When Mr. Hoover is gone, Monica plops her score on top of the piano. It's been curled up in her messenger bag for so long, it's practically a cylinder. She strolls behind the piano. "So, Shira has perfect pitch?" she asks.

"Yeah," says Felix, "we—"

"I have that," says Monica, matter-of-factly.

"You do?" says Paul. "Nice!"

Vijay sits down at the piano and plays an F. "So, if I play this note, you can tell me what it is?"

Monica licks her lips and shifts from one hip to the other. I think I see a quick, unguarded flash of panic on her face. I can see her trying to peek at the piano keys. Then she shifts her purse strap higher on her shoulder and brushes her hair back with her thumb and ring finger. She shakes her head and says, "Mine is a different kind of perfect pitch." Then she looks at me and says, "Well, who knew that my understudy had so many hidden talents."

She turns to leave, but Vijay holds up her score. "Monica," he says. "You forgot—"

She grabs it from him, and she's gone.

Chapter 16

A Toilet Flushes on F-Sharp

I lie awake thinking. I never thought of my-self as having any particular musical talent. I pounded my way through "From a Wigwam" on the piano like everybody else, and Mrs. Peabody, my piano teacher, never seemed to sense any greatness in me.

But there were those times in elementary school, when everybody was tooting out "Frère Jacques" on recorders. It drove me crazy—all the squeaks and squawks coming from the other kids' recorders, like a flock of motion-sick mourning doves. I remember wondering why it didn't bother anybody else like it bothered me.

When I learned to read music, it was like putting a name to something I already knew. Like, finding out that the "K" sound of "kangaroo" is a "K." I always knew what an E-flat sounded like. When Mrs. Peabody taught me that an E-flat was called E-flat, I just had a name for it.

But I thought it was like that for everybody.

I'm still thinking that maybe it is. Maybe Mr. Hoover is exaggerating. There are probably lots of other people with perfect pitch.

I decide to find out. When I get to homeroom the next morning, I sit next to Jeffrey Yap, the class genius, and when the bell rings, I turn to him and say casually, "Jeffrey, is the school bell a C or a C-sharp?"

I'm fully expecting him to say, "It's a C. Everybody knows that." But he doesn't. He looks at me strangely and says, "What?" like he has no idea what I'm talking about.

"Can you sing an A?" I ask, just to make sure. Jeffrey just shakes his head and goes back to double-checking his math homework.

Maybe Mr. Hoover is right. It's just me.

As the day goes on, I keep getting looks. Not obvious looks, just some glances and little grins. And with every glance, I feel the pinkness rising, from my neck to my ears, into my cheeks. And after lunch, I know that something's going on. More and more kids seem to be looking at me. I try to ignore it, but then in English, when the bell rings, Amanda James turns to me and asks, "Shira! What's that note?"

"It's a C," I answer, wondering if Jeffrey told her about my question.

Then in Spanish, Delores screams at a spider and Harry Fabian looks at me. "What note is that?" he says.

"F-sharp," I mumble.

In the hallways, everyone is looking at me. And it's not like how the barbershop quartet looked at me, sort of awed and amazed. It's the pointing, giggling kind of staring. The don't-get-too-close-it-might-be-catching kind of staring. Some kids bellow notes in my ear and walk away laughing.

"Shira has music ESP!" declares Sara Beth Cantatore, when I come into science. "She knows what any note is just by, like, knowing."

Outside, a truck is backing up, and inside, five faces stare at me. "B-flat octaves," I say.

Mrs. Franklin, our science teacher, has this way of sneezing that ends in a little squeak. Usually, everybody starts giggling. Today, they look at me. "C and F," I say.

And each time I name a pitch, my face burns redder and my heart beats faster.

Finally, Alex Jordan lets out a burp and says, "What's that?" and everyone is laughing too loud to even care about my answer. I can't stand it anymore, and I ask to go to the bathroom.

"Tell us what note the toilet flushes on!" Alex calls as I hurry out.

The bathroom door is one of those stiff springy ones. It manages to whack me from behind as I come in. A toilet flushes, and a sixth grader leaves without washing her hands. The toilet pipes shriek an A-flat. I stand in front of the mirror and examine myself, wondering if there's a way to give back my perfect pitch, to make it go away.

I hear the bathroom door open, and there's Cassie. She has a new streak in her hair. This time it's purple.

"I'm in Comp Sci, across the hall," she says. "I saw you run in here."

"I didn't run."

"Yes, you did. You very much ran. What's up?"

"They won't leave me alone," I whine. "About the perfect pitch. They're all staring at me like I'm some alien."

"So?" asks Cassie, and I can't understand how she doesn't understand.

"So, they're all looking at me, going, 'What's this note?' 'What's that note?'"

"And?"

"And I just want them to leave me alone!"

Cassie doesn't look nearly as upset for me as she should be. "So, why don't you just tell them it's a B-sharp or C, or—"

"A B-sharp *is* a C."

"Okay, fine! Whatever!" she says, and I realize maybe that wasn't the best response. "Just put up with it. It'll fade out. Somebody will always have something else to attract attention. Remember in fifth grade, when we discovered that Raquel could bend her middle finger back to touch the top of her hand?"

I nod.

"And that faded out when Ray Reich showed us how he could pop his false tooth out and put it back in."

I remember that, too. It was gross.

"So just answer their stupid questions," says Cassie. "You've got something they don't have. You're special."

"I don't want to be special. I don't want attention. I just want to blend in, be like everybody else."

"Blend in?" Cassie says, the words bouncing around the filmy white tiles. "Are you like the only kid left on this planet who wants to blend in? Haven't you noticed how hard everybody else is trying to NOT blend in? Everybody *else* wants to be noticed. Except you. You want to disappear."

I don't know what to say. Sometimes I *do* want to disappear.

"You have this crazy great hair, and you complain about it," Cassie goes on. "You have a part in the show, *and* you're understudying the lead! Do you realize how many kids . . . how much *I'd* like to have a great part in the play? Do you know what I would give to have ANYTHING that has the word 'perfect' in it?" Cassie turns to the mirror. "You know, Shira, shy girls can still be stars. And girls with purple hair can still be nobodies."

"Cassie! You're not—"

She turns around to face me. "Just go back to science and tell everybody what note Mrs. Franklin's desk drawer squeaks on. I'm going back to Comp Sci. Maybe I can make one of the programs crash, so someone will know I'm there."

She pushes open the bathroom door, and she's gone.

I'm alone again. I think about what Cassie said. About wanting a part in the play, about wanting to stand out. I haven't even been thinking about Cassie.

I wash my hands and splash my face with water. I make it back to science just in time for a fire drill. I tell anyone who wants to know that the excruciatingly loud bell is a B-flat. When the regular bell rings, and Jane Frontali looks at me, I snap, "I already told you. It's a C."

When the school day is finally over, we pour out into the hallways to pack up our things. I look for Cassie, but she's not at her locker, so I head to rehearsal, where Monica is holding court outside the music room with her friends. One of them sees me and makes her phone oink like a pig. "Shira!" she calls out. "What note is that?"

I want to tell her to leave me alone. I want to break up their little huddle and tell them that at least my perfect pitch is real, not something I say I have when I don't. I want to scream, *Stop picking on me and my special talent!* I know, it's not the strongest argument in the world, but I'm about to try it when Cassie's prediction comes true. My weirdness is suddenly put on the back burner. Because Melinda comes running down the hall, breaking into their little cluster.

"She's here!" she squeals, jumping up and down with excitement. "She's really here!"

Chapter 17

Spam

"Now?!" says Monica.

"Yes, now! Right now! In the music room!"

Monica snatches her bag off the floor with such a tug that half of its filling—lip glosses, glitter pens, hairbrushes, about six packs of gum, and three mirrors—spills out, rolling down and across the hall. Delilah scurries over, gathering it all up and handing it back to Monica. Monica stuffs everything back into her bag, and her friends troop behind her to the music room, where, apparently, something big is happening.

I start for the music room, too, having no idea who "she" is or why "she's" here. Felix is right behind me. Cassie is already sitting in the second row, with Vijay on one side and Paul on the other. I sit next to Paul. Cassie doesn't look at me.

Monica, Melinda, and their crowd sit in the back row on the far side of the room, huddling and whispering.

Mr. Hoover is standing by his desk, next to a woman in tight black pants and an off-the-shoulder sweater.

"Who's she?" I whisper to Paul.

"It's Melinda Croce's mom," Cassie answers, but she still doesn't look at me.

Just then Mr. Hoover claps for quiet. "Okay, settle down," he says.

Normally, Monica's group would be the absolute last to quiet down, but this time, Melinda sits up straight, bouncing in her chair and flapping her hands, going, "Shh, shh, shh, shh" at everyone.

"Now, I told you that our director would be joining us soon." Some squeals of delight come from the back row. "So, I'd like to introduce Mrs. Croce, Melinda's mother—" Now the back row gives a little "Me*lin*da" sing-song cheer. "—who will introduce her to you. Mrs. Croce."

Mrs. Croce walks right past Mr. Hoover, and without even a smile or a thank-you she says, "Well, boys and girls. This school musical is about to get a little more exciting . . ." She draws out the last syllable, cuing her cheer squad to give a few whoops and giggles. "Here at Hedgebrook, we can produce a typical *middle school* musical . . ." She makes a face like she's looking at some cheap dress. "Or, something *exceptional*. So, those of us on the SPAM committee—"

"SPAM?" says Cassie, a little too loudly.

"Students and Parents for the Arts and Music," says Mrs. Croce. "We on SPAM have obtained permission to bring in a very special guest director!" She balances some teensy glasses on her nose and picks up her phone. She pokes at it, scrolls, pokes again, and finally pulls up what she's been looking for.

"Our guest director," she reads, "is a multi-talented performer, and," she adds, with a head tilt and a little knee dip, "a sorority sister of mine. She has performed both off and on Broad*WAY* in original productions and revivals, and recently finished runs of . . ." She adjusts the glasses and looks harder at her screen. "*White Christmas* at the Carousel Dinner Theatre of Akron, Ohio, and *Guys and Dolls* at the Dutch Apple Dinner Theatre of Lancaster, Pennsylvania."

"Not exactly Broad*WAY*," whispers Jason.

"It has always been her dream to give back to the little people who helped her along the way."

"Is that us?" Cassie whispers to Paul.

"I guess," I say. I'm talking to Cassie even if she's not talking to me.

"We are thrilled to be able to bring her experience, enthusiasm, and im*mense* talent to Hedgebrook. May I introduce . . . *Ms. Hayley Channing!*" She waves her arm back toward the instrument room, where I guess they've stashed Ms. Hayley Channing, and as she takes her place in front, we get our first look at our new director.

She's tall and thin, with blond hair that's pinned up astoundingly high. As she looks around at all of us, I can't help noticing how the little stringy things in her neck pop out and dance around. Next to me, Felix seems to be stretching his neck out and trying to make his own stringy neck things dance, too.

Ms. Channing clasps her hands in front of her, with her bright red fingernails all lined up like little lollipops. She looks us over and says, "How beautiful! How very beautiful you are!" I glance at the back row. Monica is smiling so that even her bottom teeth show, and Melinda is clapping her hands in about a thousand tiny claps. "I am so excited to be working with Mr. . . ." She pauses. "Howard?"

"Hoover," says Paul.

"Mr. Hoover," continues Ms. Channing. "He'll be joining me as music director to put on a great show!"

"*Joining* her?" whisper-shouts Felix.

Ms. Channing looks slowly around the room. "Now, I want to get to know all of you wonderful, gifted performers. Tell me your names, and the parts you play. I already know Melinda, so let's start—"

Monica doesn't even let her finish. She jumps in, introducing herself and all of her best friends. Then Ms. Channing goes around the room, finding each one of us to be positively adorable.

Finally, she reaches our corner. Paul introduces himself as Professor Harold Hill. Vijay and Felix tell her they're in the barbershop quartet, and then Jason says he is, too.

As I start to say my name, Monica's voice sings out, "Ms. Channing! My mom says you know a lot of famous people. Could you get them to come to Hedgebrook? Please?"

Everybody erupts with chatter and the names of stars who might shortly be seen in our hallways, and it's clear my chance is gone.

"Wait!" protests Paul. But Ms. Channing is already answering.

"Now, now," she says with a low chuckle, "one day I'll tell you about all those famous people with whom I've shared the stage. But fame is not what's important. No, no, no. Let me tell you what is important." Ms. Channing closes her eyes for a moment, then begins. "Being an actor isn't about the late-night parties with the A-list. Or designer dresses or red carpets. It isn't even about winning big roles. Acting is . . ." She pauses, takes a big breath, and lets it out. ". . . *breathing*. Acting is . . ." She embraces some imaginary being in front of her. ". . . *feeling*."

I look back again, and Monica is clutching some invisible thing of her own. Vijay sits with his arms folded, perfectly still, except for his fingers, which drum impatiently. Felix's eyebrows are knit together, like he's puzzling all this out and coming up empty.

"Acting is . . . *life*," Ms. Channing concludes in a mystical whisper. She stays silent for a few seconds, leaving us all suspended in one of those clueless hold-your-breath situations, sneaking glances, wondering what happens next. I see Jason give a shrug, then scoot down in his chair to wait it out.

Then suddenly, Ms. Channing claps her hands. Jason jumps about a foot, and a pen flies out of Felix's hand, twirling and dropping to the floor before he can snatch it back.

"Warm-ups!" cries Ms. Channing. "Before we rehearse, warm-ups! Everyone, sit up! Backs straight! Up and down the scale, please. Follow me: *Do-re-mi-fa-so-la-ti-do-ti-la-so-fa-mi-re-do,*" she sings out.

She nods for us to start, and we do our best. But it's not like when Mr. Hoover leads us with big waves of his arms in the *La-de-da-de-da-de-da* of the "Minuet in G." Ms. Channing just throws out one hand and we're off. Most of us are okay on the way up but lost on the way down, moving our mouths silently like a bunch of bluefish, a few "*fa-mi-re*"s hanging pathetically in the air. We do that a bunch of times, without any better results. Then she has us sing, "*Ha-ha-ha,*" over and over again. She says it's to get the stomach muscles—called the "diaphragm"—working.

"Engage your diaphragms!" she calls out. "*Ha-ha-ha!*"

"Then what? We marry our appendixes?" whispers Vijay. Cassie snorts a laugh.

"Now, everyone up!" cries Ms. Channing. She goes over to the door and flings it open. "We will think like actors, talk like actors, walk like actors. *Allez-vous,* walk,

walk." And she waves us all out into the hallway, with Monica in the lead.

"What's going to happen to Mr. Hoover?" Felix whispers as we line up in the hall.

"What's going to happen to us?" asks Jason.

"Now, we are going to walk slowly," says Ms. Channing, almost as if she'd heard Jason's question, "heads high, hands gliding by our sides. Our necks and shoulders will be relaxed . . . no tension. No stress. We'll walk to the beat. Ready . . . go."

She starts to clap a slow, even rhythm and the first kids start to move. I get in line behind Cassie, who follows Felix, who follows Jason.

"That wasn't fair. What Monica did," says Felix, over his shoulder.

"I don't think it was on purpose," I say.

"Are you kidding?" says Cassie. "Everything Monica does is on purpose."

"Good, Melinda! Good, Monica!" calls Ms. Channing. They prance like ballerinas, turning around where the hallway dead-ends. "Heads up. Don't look down. Up! Up!"

As always, Felix follows directions, jerking his chin up, fixing his eyes ahead of him. Maybe that's why he steps on Jason's heel, pulling his shoe off. And that's why Jason stops short, and Felix trips over him. Then Cassie trips over Felix, and soon we're all in a jumble, tying up the whole line.

Ms. Channing doesn't lose her cool. She just waves her arms like a traffic cop, directing the line around our little gaggle, as Felix and Cassie get to their feet and Jason struggles to put his shoe back on.

The line snakes by us, with a few snickers, and just as we're about to get going again, Monica comes up beside me. She slows down just long enough to whisper, "I hope you enjoyed your day, Perfect Shira. I made sure to spread the word about your so-special, freaky pitch thing."

I don't know if Cassie hears, or maybe she just sees my face. But as Monica passes her, she somehow manages to get a toe in the way, and Monica takes a very un-ballerina-like lunge into Melinda. By the time Monica looks back, Cassie's standing innocently, waiting for Jason to get started.

When we're safely on our way, Cassie shoots me a look. It says, *Yes, I'm still mad at you. But I'll always have your back.* Then she starts pretend-drumming, dipping and swaying like there's music playing in her head.

"Heads up! Arms loose! Relax the shoulders! Wonnn-derful!" calls out Ms. Channing.

I hold my head up, relax my shoulders, and join the others in trying, and mostly failing, to march without tension or stress, to Ms. Channing's new beat.

Chapter 18

Call the Banana Patrol

"There's something not right about her. Her hair is scary." Felix plunks his lunch tray down next to mine. It's been a week since Ms. Channing came into our lives, and we're still trying to figure her out.

"What do you mean her hair is scary?" asks Vijay.

"It's . . . like . . . banana flavor."

"How can hair be banana flavor?" asks Paul, who's come in behind the others. "How can hair be any flavor?"

"I mean . . ." Felix gets an extra furrow in his forehead as he searches for the right comparison. ". . . like banana taffy."

"You mean it's sticky?" I ask, trying to be helpful.

"No . . ." answers Felix. "I mean the color. Haven't you ever had banana taffy? It's like some alien's idea of banana. Like hyper-fake-too-yellow yellow."

"Okay," says Vijay. "I'll call the banana patrol. But can you explain what's so terrible about hyper-banana hair?"

"I don't know," says Felix, looking sorry that he'd started this. "It's just . . ."

"Phony," says Cassie, plopping her tray down. "That's the word you're looking for. Phony."

Cassie and I used to have just one lunchtime companion—Harley H. Violet, who was present as the author of his three-inch-thick, ten-pound American history textbook, called *How We Remember*. Sometimes Cassie and I would catch up on homework or get a jump on our social studies reading. But all that has changed. Now, poor Harley stays trapped in my backpack, and we sit at a table with Felix, Jason, Vijay, and Paul. I know Cassie's still a little mad at me, so it's good that we have company. And we never run out of things to talk about now that Ms. Channing's here.

Over the past few days, Ms. Channing has done a lot of talking. She tells us we all have to be "troupers," which means working hard for the good of the play. She's taught us to say "Break a leg!" when you want to wish someone good luck, and never to "upstage" anyone, which means doing something to take the focus away from the star. She refers to us as "thespians," which means theater people, and she seems impressed by our musicianship, like we know that minor chords are "sad" and major chords are "happy."

But it's Mr. Hoover who works with the barbershop quartet and teaches the townspeople their music. He's coaching Paul and Sean on "Gary, Indiana" and Craig Horwitz, who plays Marcellus, on "Shipoopi." And he works with Paul almost every day on his songs, which are the biggest numbers in the show.

Ms. Channing spends most of her time in room 5 with Monica and the River City Ladies, but I don't hear a lot of music coming out of there—just Ms. Channing's chirpy voice. And while she's generally cheery and encouraging, every now and then I catch her off-guard—when her smile isn't fastened on and her posture isn't set—looking a little melancholy. Maybe the whole "giving back" thing isn't what she thought it would be. Or maybe there's something she's not telling us.

Today we all report to the music room for announcements. Most of the cast will stay here for "The Wells Fargo Wagon." Paul and Monica are scheduled with Ms. Channing in room 5. Monica has to leave early, so I'm going to go with them. Also, the electric piano is violently ill, making some breathy off-key sounds, like a leaky accordion, so I can stand in for the piano and give them a note or two.

After announcements, Ms. Channing calls out, "Paul! Monica! To room five with me, please!" She's waving one hand over her head in a twirly motion. Paul whispers something to her, and she adds, "Oh, and Shira."

"See you later, 'Oh-and-Shira,'" says Vijay. I give him a sideways glance and follow Paul and Monica to room 5.

"All right, ladies and gentleman," Ms. Channing says. "Let's do this marvelous scene. Paul, take it from 'You're late,' please. And Monica . . ." Ms. Channing points to the script clutched in Monica's hand. "Let's try it without the script, dear. We're aiming to be off-book for act two next week." Monica takes one last look at the page and tosses the script toward a chair. She misses, and it rolls onto the floor.

Ms. Channing sits down at the electric piano, which emits a ghostly moan.

"Oh my. I forgot." She hits the keyboard's power button to put it out of its misery and looks up at me. "Shira. Can you give Monica her starting note?"

I sing a G, which is pretty simple, but Ms. Channing says, "Brava!" and Monica shoots me a narrow-eyed look. Ms. Channing turns to Paul. "So, from 'You're late,' please. And Shira, you can prompt with pitches, and lines, if necessary."

It's necessary. Every time Paul says something, Monica looks at me and I give her a cue. This goes on until it's time for the song "Till There Was You."

"Note," says Monica, and I sing a G again.

Monica begins:

There were bells on the hill, but I never heard them ringing,
   No, I never heard them at all, till there was you.

Then she pauses, looking blank.

"There were birds in the sky . . ." I whisper. Monica glares at me, but she takes the cue and starts again.

There were birds in the sky, but I never saw them winging,
   No, I never saw them at all, till there was you.

Then her mouth opens and nothing comes out, so I prompt, "*And there was music—*"

"I know, I know!" she snaps. She fumbles through the next line, and she's a goner when she gets to "*sweet fragrant meadows of dawn and dew,*" which comes out sounding more like "*sleet flagrant memos of dog named Blue.*"

I'm waiting for Ms. Channing to say something, maybe to tell Monica she needs to spend a little more time learning the part. But she seems lost in the music, her eyes closed, her long red fingernails clicking faintly on the silent piano keys. Paul and Monica sing the last lines together:

There was love all around, but I never heard it singing,
No, I never heard it at all, till there was you.

Paul's voice sounds really sweet. It's still a little boyish, but round and full, and beautiful. And even though Monica's voice sounds a little like she's singing a fast-food commercial, they do sound good together.

After the final note, we all look at Ms. Channing, waiting for a smile or a cue. But she isn't looking at any of us. She's staring into the distance, her lips pursed and her eyelids fluttering. Then the corners of her mouth start sort of twitching, and before Monica can finish saying, "Ms. Channing, are you okay?" she lets out a little squeak, and what sounds like a sob, puts her hand over her mouth, and runs out of the room.

Chapter 19

A Double Boiler

"What just happened?" Paul asks.

"I think she was crying," I say.

We both look at Monica.

"Beats me," she says, but for a minute, we're all sort of in the same confused boat.

We walk out into the hallway. We can hear the lively chorus of "The Wells Fargo Wagon" coming from the music room.

"Do you think she's coming back?" I ask.

"I don't know," says Paul. "Should we tell Mr. Hoover?"

"How should I know?" says Monica.

"I hope it wasn't something we did," says Paul.

"I doubt it," I say. "You guys sounded really good."

"Thanks," Monica and Paul answer simultaneously, which puts them, probably for the first time ever, in a group that includes just the two of them. They both look a little freaked out.

"I guess we should look for her," I say, not knowing what else to do.

We walk up and down the hallways for a few minutes, but there's no sign of Ms. Channing. What we do come across, however, is the stage crew. They're outside room 12, at the end of a hall that's filled with half-built backdrops and what looks like the front of a house.

And there, hammering at a picket fence, is Drew. A tan rope bracelet jumps on his wrist as he hammers, and my stomach jumps in harmony with each whack.

"Hey," says Monica, stretching the word into about ten syllables and skipping across the hall to Drew. "What are you building?"

"A . . . fence," Drew says. "Somebody's fence." He calls over to Dylan Scheiner, our stage manager, "Dylan, whose fence?"

"It's . . ." Dylan consults his clipboard. "The Paroos' fence."

"That's me!" says Monica. "I'm Marian Paroo!"

"Cool," says Drew.

"That is so awesome," Monica goes on, drumming her fists with little pounds on Drew's shoulder. "You're building my fence."

I try to keep myself from staring, from imagining what it would feel like to stand so close to Drew and drum on his shoulder that way.

Paul is next to me, and I get a sense that he's just as busy as I am, puzzling out this boy-girl dance that neither of us knows the steps to.

"I didn't know you were such a good builder," squeals Monica. "And you're the best soccer player. You're like a . . . a . . . Jack of spades!"

Part of me wants to scream, *Jack of all trades! She means Jack of all trades!* Another part of me wants to catch Drew's eye and share a secret understanding. But the biggest part of me wants to sprint away and not be a witness to any of this. I end up doing none of those things. I just stand there, probably looking stupid and strange.

I feel a tap on my shoulder. It's Paul. "I'll see you inside," he says, and I nod and stay put, probably because my breathing isn't working quite right and my knees are doing that wiggly thing again.

Monica gives Drew a little tug on his arm. Her lower lip juts out in a little pout. "I wish you had a part in the show," she says. She leans on the locker behind her and gives a little toss of the head, which I think is supposed to be coy, but she tips it a little too far and thunks it on the locker. She holds her pout courageously, though, still staring into Drew's pale blue eyes and finishes, "I know you'd be great."

Dylan has disappeared for a minute, but now he's back. "Guys," he says, including me, "Ms. Channing has a headache. She says you should join the rehearsal in the music room."

Monica gives him a sour look. "Isn't that the chorus rehearsal?"

"It's the Wells Fargo scene," says Dylan.

"Do I have lines?"

Dylan flips through the pages on his clipboard. "Uh, I'm not sure. I don't think so."

"Then Shira can stand in for me."

"But—" starts Dylan.

"She's my *under*study—that's what she's *for*."

I don't like sounding like a new kitchen gadget with one hundred and one uses. Especially in front of Drew. But I don't want to stand here turning scarlet, either. I'm about to go, but Dylan isn't giving up.

"You know, Marian is center stage for this scene," he tells Monica.

That gets her attention. "She is? Why?"

"Well, Harold gives Winthrop his trumpet. It's kind of a breakthrough moment in how she sees Harold Hill."

"Breakthrough, how?"

"Well, Winthrop is her little brother, and he's really shy and self-conscious about his lisp, but he's opening up to Harold, so . . ." Monica still looks pretty blank, so Dylan goes back to Plan A. "*Center stage*, Monica. Act one finale. *Center stage.*"

"Oh, all right," she says. Then she turns to Drew. "But I'll see you after. Okay?"

Drew gives a sort of roundabout nod, and Monica flounces off for her center stage appearance, apparently forgetting all about me.

"Good job on the fence," says Dylan, and I nod in agreement. Then Dylan heads to the music room, and I'm left looking at Drew. He's looking back, the hammer in his hand, the rope bracelet circling his wrist.

"Jack of all trades!" I blurt out. Then before he can react, I dash off into the music room.

Ms. Germano has arranged the cast with the barbershop quartet on the side, the River City Ladies gathered up in a bunch, and all the townspeople lined up in rows. They've already run through the number, and everybody seems pretty charged up, bouncing with dance steps and chattering.

Monica tells her friends about what happened in room 5, and it only takes about a minute and a half until everybody knows.

"Crying?" Jason asks me. "You mean like real boo-hoo with tears and makeup smudging and everything?"

"Well, she ran out pretty fast," I say. "I felt sorry for her. She seemed really sad."

After Dylan fills Mr. Hoover in, Mr. Hoover claps his hands to get our attention.

"Okay! Ms. Channing isn't feeling well." There's some buzzing and a few giggles. "But we've got a lot to do. First, it's time to assign the solo lines. So, listen carefully." At the word "solo" the buzzing drops away. "I've tried to give at least one line to everyone who volunteered, so here goes:

"Terry, I'd like you to sing, '*I got a box of maple sugar on my birthday.*' Rashawn, '*In March I got a gray mackinaw.*'"

"What's a mackinaw?" Rashawn whispers.

"Nicole, '*And once I got some grapefruit from Tampa.*'"

"That's so spooky," says Nicole. "I did once get some grapefruit from Tampa."

"And Frankie, '*Montgom'ry Ward sent me a bathtub and a cross-cut saw.*'"

I notice that Cassie is looking at the floor, her mouth scrunched up to the side. I wonder if she volunteered for a solo.

"Okay, second verse, everyone sings, '*O-ho the Wells Fargo Wagon is a-comin' now. Is it a prepaid surprise or C.O.D?*' Then we have Edward, '*It could be curtains,*' Gianni, '*or dishes.*' And finally—this is a great line—Cassie, '*Or a double boiler!*' Then back to Terry, '*Or it could be something special just for me.*'"

He goes on to assign the third verse, which has one line that the barbershop quartet sings, but I'm still looking at Cassie. She's trying hard not to grin, but I can tell from the way she's bouncing up and down that she's excited.

"So!" Mr. Hoover declares. "When your solo line comes up, sing out! You're ordinary River City folks. We don't want perfect voices, just lots of enthusiasm. We want the audience enjoying this and laughing."

We get started, and everyone's singing about the Wells Fargo Wagon, which is kind of like an old-fashioned FedEx truck that delivers packages. Everybody's hoping for something, especially the kids in the band, who want their shiny new instruments.

O-ho the Wells Fargo Wagon is a-comin' down the street,
Oh please let it be for me

Ms. Germano has all the boys doing corny stage motions, like exaggerated underhanded swiping of fists, and the girls are tossing their imaginary skirts. Cassie is bobbing up and down with the music and singing her heart out. When it comes to the solo lines, Mr. Hoover points to each singer. A few come in on time. Rashawn and Frankie pretty much miss their cues completely. But Cassie is right on cue. "Or a double boiler!" she sings, only it comes out in a screech that sounds more like a stray cat than an enthusiastic Iowan.

In the last verse, Winthrop sings by himself:

. . . it could be
Thump'n' Thpethyal
Jutht for me.

That's the part where Marian is supposed to be beaming with pride. But Monica is just planted center stage, looking like she's waiting for a photographer to show up.

We finish with the song's rousing final lines,

O-ho, you Wells Fargo Wagon don't you dare to make a stop,
Until you stop for me.

"Okay, people!" shouts Mr. Hoover. "Good start! Soloists, rehearse your lines. And everybody, go over 'Seventy-Six Trombones' for tomorrow. There's a lot going on in that song, so know your parts!"

Everybody packs up their stuff and we pour out into the hallway. Cassie runs over to me, grabs me by both arms, and says, "I have a line! Can you believe it?"

"Of course I believe it!" I say, practically knocking her glasses off with a hug.

"Voice number seven. It says it right in the score. 'Or a double boiler!' Voice number seven."

"You're going to be great!" I say. "Now we're both somebodies, right?"

"Right, Oh-and-Shira," she says.

Vijay, Jason, and Felix come over.

"Congratulations!" says Felix.

"Nice job, Cassie," says Vijay.

"I couldn't believe it! I mean, I volunteered, but I didn't think—"

"Cassie," says another voice, and we all look at Monica. "Wow, congrats on that solo. If Hoover wants the audience laughing hysterically, he picked the perfect voice." She flashes a little half-smile and she's gone.

Cassie's face drops. She's twirling her purple streak between her fingers.

"Don't listen to her," says Vijay.

"Yeah, it's all in a day's work for a mean girl like her," says Jason.

"I know," says Cassie, but all her excitement is gone.

"Do you want to come over?" I ask her. "We could practice."

Cassie thinks for a second. She shakes her head. "No, you have work to do," she says. "You have to learn Marian's lines and all her songs and be ready to take over when Monica lands that acne commercial."

"Pepto-Bismol," suggests Felix.

"Toenail fungus," says Jason.

"I'm on it." I smile at Cassie, and add, "Voice number seven." I wave to the four of them as they head toward the front entrance, then I veer off to the side door, and my shortcut home. Down the hall I hear Jason say, "What's a double boiler, anyway?" and then Vijay's explanation, which involves the melting point of chocolate and the insulation effect of boiling water.

I'm reaching for the side door, when I hear someone say, "I'll walk with you, okay?"

Chapter 20

Glacial Erratic

It's Paul. He must have stayed behind after rehearsal to talk over some detail with Mr. Hoover.

When we open the side door, we practically step on Monica and Drew. They're sitting on the steps, shoulders touching, and Monica is whispering something in Drew's ear. Probably about Ms. Channing. Or Cassie. Or me.

We step around them, and Paul says, "See you tomorrow," as if we're all the best of friends.

Paul is walking next to me in that bouncy way of his, his script clutched tight under his arm. With each step, he lifts up and forward a little bit, like he's hearing a song in his head. The word "jaunty" comes to mind.

I look back and see Monica tap Drew on the shoulder and point at the two of us together. Then she collapses into giggles.

I snap my head forward and look ahead. I tell myself that I don't care that Drew is watching, that Monica is giggling. I tell myself that, but it's not true.

We're about halfway across the field when Paul says, "Girls like him, don't they?"

"Who?" I ask, knowing perfectly well who.

"Him. Drew." He takes a few more steps and then asks, "Do you?"

Every other kid in this school asks questions like "What's up?" or "How's it going?" The kind of questions they don't really want an answer to. How did I end up with the one kid who asks a question—that question—like he really wants an answer?

Somehow, I find a place between denial and pretending I don't know what he means. "Me? No, um, huh? What? No," I say.

Luckily, his next question is easier. "Is this really your first show?"

"Yes," I say, relieved to have an answer.

"Nobody ever told you what a great voice you have?"

I shrug.

"I bet next year you'll get the lead."

"No!" I blurt out. I feel myself freezing up, just thinking about it.

"Why not?"

"Because I'm not—" I try to find the right words. "I'm not like Monica."

"Thank goodness," says Paul.

"I mean, I don't like being the center of attention. I'd be too scared."

"Maybe you wouldn't," says Paul. He stops in front of one of the soccer goals. "I mean, I'm scared of a lot of things. Playing goalie was the scariest thing in the world. Standing there, with the ball screaming toward you? I was terrified."

I've never played goalie, but I know the feeling. I've felt it a million times. In a million places.

"I was such a bad athlete when I was a kid, they kept me out of games at recess." It's funny the way he says "when I was a kid," like that was a long time ago. "They made up rules, like if the game's started, no one can join. So, they'd throw the ball once, to say the game started. Just to keep me out."

"That's not fair," I say, but Paul just shrugs.

"I don't blame them, really," he says. "I was pretty bad."

We reach the end of the field, and he turns down Charles Street with me. "I'll walk you home," he says in a chivalrous way. I notice that jaunty way of walking again, and I look around, just to see if anybody's watching.

"The thing is, I know I goof up a lot. And I'm scared of lots of stuff, just like you. But it's different on stage," he says. "It's better. *I'm* better. And maybe it's that way for you, too."

I think that over. I wonder if it could be true. I doubt it.

"You know," says Paul, "my *abuela* seems like the most

modest person in the world. Shy, like you. But in Mexico, she was a Zarzuela star."

"Who?" I ask.

"My grandma. She sang Zarzuela. It's this great kind of opera from Spain."

We're at the end of my driveway now, and I'm about to ask why he would compare me to his grandma, when he says, "Wait! I'll sing some Zarzuela for you!" and before I know it, he's scrambling up on the giant rock that stands in our front yard. It's about fifteen feet long, flat on top, and it's shaped like a craggy lima bean. I used to hide out in its curve when I wanted to be alone.

"There's this famous song called 'No puede ser,'" he says. "It means 'It Can't Be True,' because people are saying that the girl he loves is lying."

And then he starts to sing. Out loud. In Spanish. On my rock.

His voice sounds different, more like an opera singer, kind of throaty and passionate. He's putting a lot of emotion into it, waving his arms, making a fist and shaking it in the air. And did I mention—it's very loud.

One part of me is impressed. But another part is thinking, *What if someone's passing by? What if word gets back to Monica? What if someone hears Paul singing opera right in front of my house?*

I'm so wrapped up in my thoughts, I hardly hear him finish until he asks, "Did you like it?"

"Um, yeah. Yes!" I try my best to fill my voice with enthusiasm. "It's just, I, um . . . I have a lot of homework, so . . ."

"Oh, sure. Do you mind if I stay here for a minute, though? It's not every day that you see a glacial erratic."

"A what?"

"A glacial erratic rock. It got carried by a huge glacier, probably ten thousand years ago, from way upstate or even Wisconsin. Look around. You don't see any other rock like it here, right? It just stands alone, just being itself."

By now I'm hardly surprised that he's attracted to a loner rock. Or that he's a geology fan. One more quality that scores zero points on the middle school popularity scale.

"This is a great rock," he adds, and he sits down.

So, now I have Paul sitting on my rock, where anybody passing by can see. I hear Monica's voice in my head saying, "Just because you're in a show with someone . . ." But then I remember what he told me, about being kept out of games. About how scared he was playing goalie. And if he wants to sit on this rock, I'm not going to tell him no.

"Haven't you noticed you've had a stage on your front lawn all along?"

No, I really haven't.

I notice that my mother's car is in the driveway, which means she's home. And chances are, Sophie's home, too. And that means they've been watching.

"Take your time," I say to Paul. But then I can't help myself. "Just, you probably shouldn't sing. Okay?"

"Okay," says Paul, holding a finger to his lips. "But Shira? About being like Monica? You don't have to be. In fact, I think she's jealous of you."

"That's impossible," I say.

"No it's not. But anyway, you're part of something now. You can't be shy when people are depending on you."

I give some sort of combination smile-wave and turn toward my house, where the two heads that have been peeking out the front window duck down and disappear, like magic.

Chapter 21

Turtle Brave

My mother and Sophie are both in the dining room. My mother is sorting a stack of junk mail. Sophie is leafing through a pet order catalogue, and we don't have a pet. They've obviously been watching, and my mother has even more obviously told Sophie not to mention it. But Sophie isn't very good at following instructions, so she says, "Who's that outside?"

"Who's who?" my mother says, playing dumb, but shooting Sophie a we'll-talk-later glance.

"The boy outside, sitting on our rock. The one who was singing."

"Somebody from school," I answer. I can play dumb as well as she can.

"Oh," says my mother, taking a look outside like it's the first time. "Is he a friend from the show?"

"Yes," I say.

"What's he doing?" asks Sophie.

Paul is sitting on the edge of the rock, his script spread out on his lap. He's going over one of his songs, probably "Seventy-Six Trombones," judging from the arm motions.

"I think he's rehearsing," I say.

"What part is he playing?" asks my mother.

"Harold Hill."

She looks out the window again and smiles. "I always got a crush on the leading man in the school play . . ."

"Mom. I don't have a crush on him."

"He's too little to have a crush on," says Sophie.

"No, he looks sweet," says my mother. "Should I invite him in?"

"No!" I answer. "You should not invite him in! He's going home. Soon."

"He must like you," says my mother, glancing out the window again, "to walk you home, and serenade you. And sit on a rock."

"Mom," I say, "it's not about me . . . it's about . . . the rock. It's some kind of rock. Eccentric or something." I want this idea of hers that Paul is my lovestruck Romeo to be nipped in the bud.

"He was singing to you," says Sophie.

"He wasn't singing *to* me. He was singing this song. It's Mexican. Or Spanish, but he was just showing me. Not singing to me."

"You know, when Dad first asked me out in high school . . ."

Now it's Sophie and I who exchange looks. We've heard the story so many times—how it took two years for my dad to get my mom to go out with him, and then she finally saw the light and they got married right after college. She's convinced that whatever happened to her is bound to happen to us. I take my script and start up the stairs. I call to her over my shoulder, "Just to review, there is no way that I'm marrying Paul Garcia."

"All right. I believe you," calls my mother, but I hear her whisper to Sophie, "You never know."

Once I'm in my room, I text Cassie, "Practicing your part?" I get back a smiley face and some musical notes.

I look down through my eyebrow window at Paul. It's hard to believe that the things that are so hard for one person can be so easy for another. My hiding place is his stage. And another kid's recess is Paul's nightmare.

My parents always say they're waiting for me to come out of my shell. I've always thought of it like a bird hatching, with the bright sun in its eyes, and that poor little bird wanting to climb back into the egg but realizing that once you've hatched, there's no going back, the shell is broken. But maybe it's more like a turtle coming out of its shell. It can choose its moment, when it's feeling brave, and try it out. If it picks the wrong time, then *zoop*, it's back in, until it's ready to try again. There's no final decision, just a try. Maybe it wouldn't be quite as hard as I thought.

"Is he still there?" It's Sophie, standing in my doorway.

"Yup."

"How long do you think he'll stay?"

"I don't know."

"You think he'll stay all night?"

"Of course not."

"Love can make you do strange things."

"Stop it," I snap. "I told you. I don't have a crush on him and he doesn't have a crush on me."

"Do you have a crush on anyone else?" I must hesitate for just a fraction of a second too long, because Sophie jumps on it. "Who?"

"Nobody."

"Oh, come on."

"Okay, maybe I do. But it's none of your business and nothing's going to happen, anyway, because there's this other . . . never mind."

"Doesn't know you're alive, huh?"

I glare at her, wondering why little sisters have to be so perceptive.

"It's okay," she says. "Love triangles are cool."

"What love triangle?"

"Well, Paul likes you, but you like somebody else, and that person likes another person. Wait." She starts drawing in the air. "That would make a love rectangle." After a few seconds of thought, she gives up on her air diagram and shrugs. "Anyway, Paul definitely likes you."

"Go away."

"Okay, but if you need me, you know where to find me."

I hear the door to her room close. I take out my script. I need to get started. I go over Marian's scene with her mother one more time. I sing through "My White Knight," softly enough that Sophie can't hear. I think about what Paul said, that Monica is jealous of me. That can in no way be true.

Then I look outside.

Paul is still there. He jumps off the rock and looks toward the house. I know he can't see me. But just as he's turning to go, he waves. Not at me. He's looking at one of the downstairs windows. And I realize with a sinking feeling that he's waving at my mother, who must be waving cheerily back.

Chapter 22

Jade Marimba Teal

At rehearsal the next afternoon, Ms. Chan-
ning hushes everyone. "Mr. Hoover tells me you were
troupers in my absence yesterday," she says. "Sadly, my
artistic temperament makes me prone to what the French
call 'la migraine.'" She holds one finger to her forehead.
"In English, migraines."

"My mother gets migraines," whispers Cassie. "She
doesn't break into tears first."

"Maybe French people do," says Jason.

"So, thank you, my thespians," she goes on, "and your
reward is, today we order our costumes!"

There's a general squeal among the girls, and even the
boys are suddenly listening. Ms. Channing starts handing
out forms and pamphlets. "Find your part and fill in the
blanks. Townspeople, just sizes, please. We'll assign patterns for you, to get a diverse color scheme. Female leads
and name parts, you have a few color choices. Harold Hill,
we need sizes for your suit and bandleader's uniform. Let's
not take too long. We have a play to rehearse!"

I flip to the boys' side of the form. The "boys-playing-men" will wear jackets, pants, and suspenders, and the "boys-playing-children" will tuck their pants into long socks to make "knickers." Most of the boys get band uniforms. All Jacey Squires and the rest of the barbershop quartet get is a particularly ugly plaid jacket, bow tie, and hat.

"A reminder!" Ms. Channing calls out. "I see some gum chewing going on. Out please! In the wastebasket!" I glance over at Monica, who reluctantly takes a piece of gum out of her mouth. She pats her pockets, then tries unsuccessfully to dig a finger into one of them. She does a helpless little flappy dance, waving pathetically until Melinda runs up to accept the gum in her open palm and race it over to the wastebasket.

"Ugh," I say, imagining the feel of Monica's spit-laced gum in my hand.

"New jeans rule," says Cassie. "If you can't fit a gum wrapper in your pocket, they're too tight."

I go back to my order form. "What size jacket would I be? It comes in boys' sizes ten to twenty."

"I don't know," Cassie says. "Ask Felix."

"I don't know," says Felix. "My mother buys me stuff. Ask Jason."

"I left twenty husky behind last year," says Jason. "I don't think I'll even fit into these things."

As if she hears us, Ms. Channing calls out, "If you don't

know your size, Ms. O'Flanahan can measure you in the instrument storage area."

I hadn't noticed Ms. O'Flanahan sitting in the far corner. Ms. O works in the main office. She has these long, long nails—not the decorated kind, with red polish or little moon-and-star decals. Ms. O'Flanahan's nails are just really long, and kind of yellow.

Felix, Jason, and I look at each other and quickly fill in a size box, figuring we'd rather guess at our sizes than end up slashed by a tape-measure-wielding Ms. O. Paul seems to know his size, and it takes him just a few seconds to fill out his form.

Meanwhile, Monica is eagerly flipping through the brochure. "I get three changes," she tells Melinda. "Help me pick." Melinda pulls Delilah over and they huddle with Monica, giggling.

"Gross," says Monica, pointing to a picture.

"Gross," says Melinda.

"So gross," adds Delilah.

"Sometimes their vocabulary just knocks me out," says Vijay, who's come up behind us.

"Dazzling, isn't it?" says Cassie, slowly moving her hand to cover the number she's filled in under "size."

"This one's covered with tulips and garlic," says Monica, pointing at a picture.

"Order it in purple," says Delilah, and they laugh.

"They're tulip bulbs, sweetie," says Ms. Channing, joining their pod for a quick look at the picture. "It's a country look. But there are two patterns. You can choose the other one." Then she adds, "Now, just another minute, ladies."

Monica finally decides and marks her choices. On her way to hand it over to Ms. Channing, she pauses in front of me. "You're going to look so cute in that mustache," she says.

She marches over to hand in her form, and I do my best to ignore her. Ms. Channing is busy arranging the papers in a neat pile and stuffing them into a big envelope. She holds it up, calling out, "I need a volunteer to run this down to the main office."

When Felix scratches his nose, she happily hands him the package. "Thank you . . ." She trails off, clearly forgetting Felix's name.

After Mr. Hoover makes today's announcements, we break up into our assigned rehearsals.

Paul and I get to room 5 first. We're going over "Marian the Librarian." I'm supposed to show Monica the choreography we did with Ms. Germano, but Ms. Channing says she has "a vision" for this scene, so she's sent Ms. Germano to work with the River City Ladies.

We have to wait for Monica, who's made a detour to the girls' room. And when she finally comes in, she's annoyed. More than annoyed. She's incensed. She's holding her makeup bag in front of her. It's small and log-shaped and unzipped down the middle, with everything inside spilling out like the filling in an over-stuffed potato.

"My Jade," she says. "Somebody took my Jade."

"What's a Jade?" asks Paul, and he looks at me, like maybe I can translate.

"It's makeup," I whisper.

The library patrons are starting to come in, but Monica is in no mood to start rehearsal. "It's not just makeup," she snaps. "It's *Jade*. It has its *own store* in the mall."

"Maybe you left it somewhere," suggests Paul.

"I didn't *leave* it anywhere. Someone took it." Her lower lip sticks out in a little pout. "I didn't even use it yet. It's this perfect shade. Marimba Teal."

Paul looks totally lost. "Why would anybody want to take your lipstick?"

"It's *eyeliner!*"

When Ms. Channing makes her entrance, she can instantly tell that Monica's upset. Maybe it's her performer's sixth sense, or maybe it's the angry red color that Monica has turned. Probably that.

"Monica. Sweetie," says Ms. Channing. "What's wrong?"

Monica tells her about her great loss, and Ms. Channing tilts her head and smiles.

"Now, Miss Marian," she says, drawing Monica to her and resting her head on what looks like a very sharp collarbone, "we're all behind you. We understand. Don't we,

Shira? Don't we, Paul?" She reaches her hand out to Paul, who gives a nod, but stays put in his chair, defeating Ms. Channing's plans for a group hug.

"Of course we do," Ms. Channing says. "But what do theater professionals do in times of trouble?" Monica clearly doesn't have a clue. "They carry on. Missing Jade or no missing Jade, what do they do?"

She waits, until Monica mutters an unconvincing "They carry on."

"Good!" says Ms. Channing. "So, let's put all this negative energy behind us, and do this wonderful scene."

Monica stands, her jaw still clenched, and waits for instructions. There's a new electric piano that sounds more like a kiddie toy piano, but at least it plays, and Ms. Channing starts the "Dum—da-duh-duh-duh" introduction. I lead Monica around, trying to do what Ms. Germano showed us at the last rehearsal. Paul starts singing, but Ms. Channing keeps calling out instructions to Monica, like "Stay resistant, but coy! Chin up! Strong woman!" Monica does her best, but her coy resistance looks more like a spoiled mean girl sneer.

The other kids circle around, like we did with Ms. Germano, but Ms. Channing doesn't look happy. She stops playing and stands, gathering up the library patrons and giving them new instructions.

Soon they're zigzagging to the back of the room, then up front again, which works okay until we add Marian to the mix and she runs smack into the zigzag parade. That's probably because she's racing away from Harold with a paranoid over-the-shoulder glare like he's some kind of mass murderer.

Ms. Channing seems only a little discouraged, though, and after a few more tries, she assures everyone that next time we'll smooth out the rough edges.

We gather up our things. The next part of rehearsal is "Seventy-Six Trombones," in the music room. Monica takes one more look into her makeup bag for her missing Jade, then stuffs it angrily into her tote bag and pushes open the door to the hallway.

I'm about to follow, when I hear a scream.

Paul and I both rush out the door to see what's happened. A group of kids is bunched around the locker that's directly opposite room 5, pointing and giggling. Delilah and Melinda have heard Monica's cry and come running.

Monica yanks a pack of tissues out of her bag, feverishly trying to wipe something off the locker. By now, a whole bunch of kids has seen it, and everyone's whispering and laughing.

Monica turns and glares at Paul and me. "You! Both of you! You did this! It had to be you!"

I look to see what everyone's staring at. Finally, I see it. It's a little bit smudged from Monica's scrubbing, but it's clear enough. On the locker, in a shiny blue-green that I instantly guess is Jade Marimba Teal, is a neatly drawn heart, and inside is a phrase that someone obviously means as a killer blow to Monica's well-honed reputation.

"Monica & Paul 4 Ever"

Chapter 23

Crashing Cymbals

Paul seems just as spooked by the words on the locker as Monica. But he has to shake it off. Coming up is the "Seventy-Six Trombones" rehearsal, and that's Paul's biggest number.

In the music room, everyone is laughing about the Marimba Teal mystery message, but Mr. Hoover does his best to tamp down the excitement.

"Townspeople!" calls Ms. Germano. "Get into your groups, please. Barbershop in the corner. River City Ladies, Mayor Shinn, stage right!"

I huddle with the barbershop quartet. "Who could possibly have written that?" asks Vijay.

"Somebody who knew how to push Monica's buttons," says Jason.

"Places everyone!" calls out Mr. Hoover. "Seventy-Six Trombones!"

"I tried playing the trombone in fourth grade," says Jason. "Turns out I was allergic to the metal. I got this scaly rash all over my hands."

"Jason," says Felix. "Too much information."

When we're all in place, Mr. Hoover quiets us down. "Seventy-Six Trombones" is the most famous song in the show. It's the one that everyone's heard. I'm nervous for Paul, but I remember what he said on the walk home. I hope what he said about being onstage is true.

"All right," calls Ms. Channing. "This is the centerpiece of the show. We all know the song. It's Harold Hill's calling card. He's already convinced all you citizens that there's 'trouble' in River City. Now he has to convince you that the cure is forming a boys' band. He has to show you the magic!" She waves her hands in the air like she's doing the hokey-pokey. "Now, boys and girls, I want you to listen to every word, then be ready for your cue. You come in after he sings 'A full octave higher than the score!'"

She waves at Mr. Hoover to get started, and Paul takes his place. The whole cast surrounds him. The song starts with a kind of rhythmic talking, and Paul knows every word.

May I have your attention, please?
Attention, please!
I can deal with this trouble, friends,
With a wave of my hand, this very hand!
Please observe me if you will,
I'm Professor Harold Hill,
And I'm here to organize the River City Boys Band!

At first no one is really paying attention. A few kids

are bouncing to the rhythm, but in a joking around way, like they're waiting for something to tease Paul about, or to make fun of this whole thing. But as Paul gets into the song, something changes.

Maybe it's the rhythm, maybe it's the words that come tumbling out of Paul's mouth, maybe it's the way his hands point and pull us in and shape instruments in midair. He's totally comfortable, reeling off his sales pitch in rhyme. "Well Professor Harold Hill's on hand, and River City's gonna have her Boys Band . . ." until the rhythm changes to a parade beat, and he takes us all with him.

And you'll see the glitter of crashing cymbals.
And you'll hear the thunder of rolling drums;
The shimmer of trumpets—Tah-ta-ra!

It's like we're not Hedgebrook Middle Schoolers anymore but townsfolk of River City. Suddenly, I can see what he was talking about that day on the rock. This is what Paul does better than anything. This is where he's meant to be.

And then Mr. Hoover plays the intro—five notes up and five notes down, and then a G, and Paul starts to sing. "Seventy-six trombones led the big parade / With a hundred and ten cornets close at hand . . ."

It's a melody that everybody's heard a million times. It's a tune that gets you marching and picks you up, full of confidence and spirit, but there's also something about it that seems to be speaking just to me. It's like I've heard it before, just recently, but I can't put my finger on it.

But more than the song, more than the melody, there's Paul. His voice and his energy. Harold Hill is a salesman, and he's selling excitement, anticipation, and that thing that Paul has so much of, enthusiasm. When he sings "Seventy-six trombones caught the morning sun," I can practically see those trombones glinting away. "Clarinets of ev'ry size and trumpeters who'd improvise a full octave higher than the score."

The piano takes over, and Mr. Hoover catches Paul's excitement—his hands flying up and back to the keyboard. He's hardly looking at the music; he seems to know it by heart. Kids are marching along with Paul or doing a kind of chorus line dance kick.

Unfortunately, everybody's so busy dancing, we all miss the cue. Ms. Channing throws her arms up and waves to Mr. Hoover, and it all comes to a dead stop.

There are a few "whoa"s and "awesome"s coming from the group, and Mr. Hoover stands up and leads a round of applause for Paul, who gives a modest shrug. Somebody starts up a cheer of "Paul! Paul! Paul!" and everybody seems to be in a good mood, except Monica. She's standing by the door, the only one not cheering.

"People, that was your cue!" Ms. Channing cries, her voice crackling with irritation. She turns to Mr. Hoover and says, "Take it from where we left off. Townspeople, at my cue you come in. Ready . . ." and she points to Mr. Hoover.

This time we come in on cue, but it's a little like Ms. Channing has let the air out of the balloon. The magic is gone. For now.

We start up singing again, and slow it down, and spend some time putting the pieces together. But as I look over at Paul, I realize that Monica hasn't been the only one looking through people, pretending they're not there. I've been looking right through Paul all this time. I haven't seen him at all.

Chapter 24

A Thousand Kisses Shy

The next day, Ms. Pappalardo is absent. I guess they couldn't find a substitute, or at least not a substitute willing to teach health to seventh graders, because there's a sign on the door sending us all to the auditorium for study hall. The teacher on duty is Mr. Gables, one of the PE teachers. I get the feeling he didn't do much studying when he was a kid, so he doesn't expect much from us now.

I sit about three-quarters of the way back in the second seat, leaving one open for Cassie. Health is one of the classes we have together. I take out *How We Remember*, and I'm kind of looking forward to spending some time with Cassie and Harley H. Violet like we used to do.

After a couple of minutes, she plunks down in the seat next to me.

"There's something we need to talk about," she says.

I sit up and give her all my attention. I don't want her to think ever again that I'm too busy feeling sorry for myself to listen.

"Is it about Wells Fargo?" I ask.

"No, this is much more important."

"Okay," I say.

"Here it is: Let's say Monica gets violently ill, you play Marian, and you kiss Paul."

"Whoa. Wait a minute." This isn't going where I thought it was going at all. "First of all, Monica is not getting violently ill . . ."

"You never know. There are some nasty viruses out there. Anyway, theoretically, here's the question: Does that count as a first kiss? I mean officially, your first kiss?"

"Cassie! No! And keep your voice down," I add in a whisper.

"Come on, Shira. Don't answer so fast. This is important. It's totally possible, and I can't decide . . . does it count?"

If it were anybody else asking me this, I'd just say they were crazy and walk away. But it's Cassie. We've always talked about everything and imagined a million times what our first kisses would be like.

Sometimes I picture it during the summer. On a beach, maybe. I'd meet some boy who was cute and a little shy, not pushy or full of himself. Other times, I imagine someone a little goofy—with curly hair like mine or a lopsided smile. Or someone with beautiful green eyes. And lately, I have to admit, I picture him looking a lot like Drew.

"Of course, I'm assuming you're not hiding anything," says Cassie. "I mean, you haven't snuck in a kiss when I wasn't looking?"

"Cassie!" I glare at her.

"So?" asks Cassie. "What do you think?"

I picture Paul Garcia and me, on the bridge, in front of all those people. No beach. No crashing waves. No Drew.

"No, of course it wouldn't count," I say quickly. "I'd be playing a part. It wouldn't be me kissing Paul, it would be Marian kissing Harold Hill."

"Well, *you* might be playing a part, but I don't know about him . . ."

"What?"

"Oh, come on. You know Paul has a crush on you."

"He does not," I say. "Cassie, it wouldn't count—"

"And you would be kissing him. I mean, technically, it would be lips on lips, you know, physically, it's"—she smacks her lips together—"a kiss."

"What kiss?" asks Vijay. I guess we've been so involved in our discussion that we didn't hear Vijay and Jason coming down the aisle. They plunk into the seats behind us, each one trying to get his chair to make a bigger burp sound.

"Nothing," I say quickly.

"No way," says Jason. "You were saying something about a kiss."

"What kiss?" says Felix, appearing from nowhere.

"What are you guys all doing here?" I ask.

"Somebody spilled ball bearings all over the floor in science, so they sent us here. We had to hold on to the desks to even make it to the door."

"We were talking about stage kisses," says Cassie. "If Shira—" I manage a swift kick to Cassie's ankle. "Say, hypothetically . . ."

Vijay sits up straight, looking excited. "A hypothetical! Neat!"

"If . . . a *person* was to kiss *another person* in a play. And if, say, that person hadn't ever been kissed before . . ."

"Hypothetically," Vijay says.

"Wait. How can you hypothetically kiss somebody?" asks Jason.

"The situation is hypothetical, not the kiss," says Vijay.

"Should we be talking?" asks Felix. "Are we going to get in trouble?"

"Oh, please," says Jason. "Mr. Gables is deep into his Fantasy Football right now."

"Okay," says Felix. "So this hypothetical kiss . . ."

"Right," says Cassie. "So, hypothetically, if this person has to kiss somebody in a play, does it count as a first kiss?"

I wonder how much crud I'd end up with on my knees and in my hair if I just ducked under the seats and crawled to safety.

"Interesting question," says Vijay, scratching his chin.

"The kiss is in the script, right? I mean, it's not like these two necessarily want to kiss each other."

"Well . . . one of them might—" says Cassie. I kick her again. "And one might not," she adds.

"That makes it a little trickier," says Vijay. "Let me think about this."

"Is it a real kiss?" asks Jason. He's leaning so far forward he's draped halfway over the chair into the one next to me. "I mean, is there tongue and everything?" I hear a creak-like sound and I realize it's coming from me.

"So," says Vijay, ignoring Jason's question, "there are a few scenarios. Neither one wants to kiss. Both want to kiss. Or one of them does, but the other is just acting. Now, does that affect the question . . . ?"

While he pauses to ponder that, Jason says, "I'd count it. If it were me, I'd definitely count it."

"Even if you're just playing a part?" asks Felix. "I mean, if you're playing a part, is it really you doing the thing?"

"Me? Are you kidding? I'd count it any way at all," says Jason. "But we're talking about Shira and Paul, right?"

"No!" I say. "We're talking about a totally, *totally* hypothetical situation."

"Well, yeah. But if Monica eats an E. coli burger and she's throwing up all over the place, and you end up playing her part . . ." says Jason.

"I was thinking more malaria, but yeah," Cassie answers.

"It doesn't matter!" I protest. "Because it's not going to happen."

"Yeah, you're right. It's probably Monica that gets the old smoochola anyway," says Jason.

"And it won't be *her* first . . ." adds Cassie.

"But it's an interesting question," says Vijay. "I would say the answer is, it depends how you feel. How it feels. The kiss, I mean. That's when you'd know if you count it or not."

"Wow," says Felix. "You should start an advice column or something."

"My door is always open," answers Vijay.

Chapter 25

Spotlight

•

That afternoon, Dr. Leeds has scheduled a "mini-tech rehearsal." He's recruited the lighting crew from the computer coding club, and he wants them to get the hang of using the lights. Mr. Hoover wraps up rehearsal early and we're all encouraged to go to the auditorium to provide the lighting crew with real live people to practice on.

In the hallway, a small clutch of girls surrounds Monica. She's obviously depositing some little droplet of gossip.

"So, Danny Pruitt is out!" she says.

"Danny Pruitt?" repeats Delilah. Her face hovers in an odd shock-smile-frown as she tries to figure out what reaction Monica expects of her.

Vijay and Felix come up behind me to see what's happening.

"Danny Pruitt is out of what?" asks Vijay. Monica casts a sideways glance at Vijay, trying to decide if stooping to answer him will demote her in any way. She compromises by directing her answer to her friends.

"Obviously, he's out of the show," she says.

"Why?" asks Felix.

Monica puts two shiny blue squares of gum into her mouth and gives him the you're-just-too-stupid-to-understand-aren't-you look. "Because Tommy has to dance," she says.

"Wait. Who's Tommy?" asks Felix. "I thought we were talking about Danny."

"Danny is *playing* Tommy," Monica answers. She gives her gum a sharp snap. "He has to be able to dance. And Danny can't."

"So why did he get the part?" asks Vijay.

"Because he could dance."

"Wait," says Felix. "I thought you said—"

"*Then.* He could dance *then*, but he can't now."

"Why not?" asks Vijay.

"Because he broke his leg."

"We could've saved a lot of time if you'd just started with that," mumbles Felix.

Cassie and Jason have come over and I fill them in. "Danny Pruitt broke his leg."

"How did he break it?" Cassie asks Monica.

"He was chasing Eric Schmidt down the stairs and tripped on his pants."

"Eric's pants or his own pants?" asks Jason.

"His own!" snaps Monica. "But the *important* thing . . ."

Poor Danny. His broken leg is already shoved to the back

burner. "The *important* thing, is that Drew Jensen is going to play Tommy!"

I confess, my stomach does a little whirly-turn when she mentions Drew.

"But what about soccer?" asks Delilah. She seems to know an awful lot about Drew's schedule. If I were Monica, I'd be a little suspicious.

"The coach said he could miss some practices. And Ms. Channing says it's worth having him in the cast, even if he can't come to every rehearsal. He's a perfect Tommy."

"So, the world is saved," says Cassie.

"And Drew will be Melinda's boyfriend!" says Delilah.

"In the *show*!" snaps Monica. "He'll be playing her boyfriend *IN THE SHOW*."

"Du-uh!" chirps Delilah, in a two syllable, self-put-down way. "I mean, everyone knows that you and Drew are going out." I try to ignore the jab that goes through my stomach and down to my toes.

"It's almost enough to make me wish I'd gotten Melinda's part," says Monica with a wistful sigh. "It would be so right to be in his arms, onstage and off." Delilah tries out a misty-eyed look, but there's a little twist in her face that suggests she's really trying to keep her gag reflex under control. Monica goes on, "Still, there are times when you have to choose between personal happiness and career. And now I have to make the sacrifice and put career first."

"It must be so hard, juggling so much talent and popularity," mutters Cassie.

Monica makes a little shooing away motion. "Aren't you late for Dr. Leeds's mini thing?" she says.

"You're not going?" I ask.

"Ms. Channing and I will be doing some character work. So, no, I'm not going." I wonder if character work means learning her lines.

Cassie takes me by the arm and pulls me into the auditorium. Jason, Vijay, and Felix have already found seats. We sit down with them and wait to see what happens next.

Two of the lighting crew kids are manning some spotlights, which look like overgrown desk lamps. A couple others are playing around with the switches in the wings, making the stage light up in different colors.

"Wow," says Jason. "Pretty razzle-dazzly, huh?"

A few stage crew kids are working on the sets, turning red, then white, then blue as they hang some backdrops and position the sets for the Paroos' house and the little town of River City.

I feel Cassie's elbow in my ribs and she points. Up on stage, Drew is sanding the corner of something that looks like a nursery school teeter-totter. He stands up, puts his hands on his hips, and looks it over.

Then Dr. Leeds calls out, "All right! Attention, everyone." He's gripping a script in one hand, holding it up in the air. "Full tech won't be for a few weeks, but I've designed a few scenes I'd like to try out. Thanks to all of you for helping us here." I glance around the auditorium. It looks like most of the cast has decided that hanging out on the school's front steps or going down to 7-Eleven for a Slurpee is more fun than coming to Dr. Leeds's rehearsal.

"So, I've asked the stage crew to have the footbridge ready. Is that it?" he calls up to Drew. "You, up there . . ." Drew lifts his head, a sandy wave of hair falls over his forehead. "Yes, you. Is that the footbridge?"

Drew shrugs and nods and turns the teeter-totter over. And there it is—an arch-shaped footbridge.

"Good," continues Dr. Leeds. "Let's start with that scene. The SPAM committee has bought these two beautiful new spotlights for us, and this is a perfect scene for them. Are you ready back there?"

The two kids behind those jumbo-sized lamps nod confidently.

"So . . . Marian? Harold Hill?" He looks around the room. "We need Marian and Harold Hill for this scene. Are they here?"

"Monica's with Ms. Channing," says Cassie.

"And Paul is at the dentist," says Vijay. "He's coming late."

"Maybe we should start with another scene," suggests Dylan, flipping through the papers on his clipboard.

"No, no," Dr. Leeds sighs. "Let's just use stand-ins until they get here. All we need is a couple of bodies up there."

"Shira's here," says Jason in a loud voice. "She's the understudy for Marian."

"Good," says Dr. Leeds. "Sharon, let's go. And you," he says, pointing at Drew. "Just stay up there and stand in for Harold Hill."

I'm halfway out of my chair, and I freeze.

"Go," says Cassie.

"Go on, Sharon," says Jason.

"I'm not—" Drew starts, but Dr. Leeds cuts him off, shaking his head and pinching the bridge of his nose.

"I know it's not your part, but we need—a body double, like in the movies."

"Could he be my body double?" says Jason. "In gym?"

"What's your name?" Dr. Leeds asks Drew.

"Drew," he says. He runs his fingers through his hair to push back that wave.

"Okay, Drew. You just have to stand up there with this pretty girl here. I'm sure you can do that." I can't imagine what kind of training Dr. Leeds could have had that left out the part about not saying embarrassing things like that about seventh graders.

I climb the steps up the side of the stage on jiggly knees and make my way over to the bridge.

"Do you know the lines?" asks Dr. Leeds.

"Yes," I say, because I've pretty much got the whole script down, and the songs, too. But Drew shakes his head and shrugs.

"Okay . . ." Dr. Leeds flips through his script and squeezes his eyebrows. "No lines then, we'll just do the blocking. Step onto the bridge." Drew and I are on opposite sides. I stare at his hand, resting gently on the railing. I step up onto the bridge and look at the stage floor peeking through the bridge's wooden slats. I start to walk toward the middle.

"No-no-no-no! Just one step in," yells Dr. Leeds. I jump back off the bridge and so does Drew. He gives me a pretend-frightened look, but any response from me is about a thousand levels of functioning beyond what I'm capable of.

Dr. Leeds directs us more clearly, "First you're going to be apart, and *then* you come together. So first, let's try two spots . . ." A light hits me in the eyes and I have to cover them with my hands.

"Okay, so maybe that's a bit too strong. Doug, Molly, lower them just a notch." Then another voice says, "Shira." I look out but get blinded again, and the voice says, "It's Mr. Hoover. Why don't you sing a verse of 'Till There Was You,' so the lighting people can get an idea of the timing. What do you think?"

I can't see Mr. Hoover, and I'm frozen, one foot on the

bridge, one off. I know the song. I know the starting note and the words and the melody, but I can hardly open my mouth.

"Shira?" says Mr. Hoover, and all I can do is shake my head.

"You know, on second thought," he says, seeing me frozen, "I'll just play the song. Let them concentrate on your direction."

"Fine," says Dr. Leeds. "Just one step onto the bridge, both of you."

I take a shaky step up. Mr. Hoover starts playing the music to "Till There Was You" softly.

"Now move in toward each other. Drew, you too, and we'll follow you until it's just one spot, in the middle of the bridge."

My heart is pounding and I'm glad there's a railing to hold on to. We each take a slow step, getting closer and closer to the middle, as the song plays. "Okay, move the spot, move it with them," Dr. Leeds continues. "Good, slow, it looks beautiful. Now, Drew, you step up to her, put your arm around her." I feel his T-shirt brush up against my arm. Then I feel his hand on my shoulder.

I try to stay relaxed, to pretend it's the same as when Jason and Vijay drape their arms over me when we're singing "Lida Rose." But it's not the same. Not at all.

"Don't you think they should look at each other, Tim?"

I realize that Tim is Mr. Hoover, who says, "Good idea. Turn toward each other. Hold both her hands, Drew." As the music reaches the end of the song, we face each other and hold hands. Drew's are warm. I can't look up into his face. The best I can do is focus on the V-neck of his light blue T-shirt. I wonder if he's looking at me. I wonder just how sweaty my hands feel, or if they're shaking. They must be shaking. I wonder what he could possibly be thinking.

Mr. Hoover reaches the end of the song, and Dr. Leeds calls out to his crew, "Okay, hold the spot right there. And that's when . . . they . . . kiss," and I think my heart does actually skip a beat.

Drew's face is so close to mine, I can see how his eyelashes blink away a stray piece of blondish hair.

But then I hear a voice, a shrill voice, coming from the back of the auditorium.

"What's going on?" We drop our hands and look out into the glare of lights. "Why are they up there? What are you *doing*?!" All I can see is a blurry figure striding down the aisle. An angry, blurry figure. It's Monica. "Turn off that spotlight!"

The light goes off.

"No, no, no!" Dr. Leeds calls out. "We need the spot back on!"

The light flashes back to blinding life. "Monica," says Dr. Leeds, "I beg your pardon, but we were working on—"

"That's my scene!" shouts Monica.

"I know, dear," he says, putting on his psychologist calm voice, "but you were working with Ms. Channing and we needed to get started."

Monica marches toward the stage and starts to climb the stairs. I'm not waiting until she gets any closer. I race down the other side and into the third row, next to Cassie, my heart beating like someone turned the knob up to max. Monica grabs Drew's hand.

"All right," she says, "somebody get me my script so we can do the scene."

"The other girl said she knew the scene," Dr. Leeds says. I think a stray red spotlight hits Monica's face. Either that or she's really mad.

"Here, take mine," says Dylan. As he hands it up to her, Ms. Channing arrives. And Paul, too. "Oh my, it's the foot-bridge!" she says. "Paul, go up and join Monica."

Paul makes his way up to the stage, taking Drew's place, and it's the first time I see anything but an adoring look from Monica toward Ms. Channing. In fact, it's a full-fledged icy glare. Jason slides way down in his seat, stifling a wave of giggles he doesn't want Paul to hear.

"Now that we're all here, let's run the scene through," says Ms. Channing.

Dr. Leeds shrugs.

"Take it from, 'You're late,'" calls out Mr. Hoover.

I take a deep breath, trying to make my heart slow down to its normal rate. Just a minute ago it had been me up there. And Drew. And almost, a kiss.

I don't look at Cassie, even though she's sitting right next to me. I certainly don't look to see where Drew has gone. As Monica starts reading her lines, Cassie leans toward me.

"It would have counted," she whispers. "It *definitely* would have counted."

Chapter 26

One Door Closes

The next day, I avoid my usual route from lunch to English. That would take me past Drew's locker. And as much as I've hoped to catch a glimpse of him in the past few weeks, the last thing I want today is to run into him.

I try to remind myself that what happened was at least three steps away from reality. We were stand-ins for people who are playing other people who aren't even real to begin with. He probably didn't even think about it after we got off the stage. Or if he did, it was probably just how weird and embarrassing it was that he almost had to kiss this frizzy-haired girl he didn't even know. But standing so close to him was real, and me freezing up was real, and I don't know what I would say if I saw him now. Not that I've ever known what to say before, but this is like a hundred times worse.

My non-Drew's-locker route takes me past my own locker, so I stop to put away Harley H. Violet and to look over Ms. Schneider's comments on my 1650 farm project. They're written in red and practically illegible.

"Massachusetts Bay Colony," a voice says. I look up and barely manage not to drop everything on the floor. It's Drew. I stare and nod. Somehow, despite my careful plans, here he is. He points to Ms. Schneider's scrawl. Her handwriting is instantly recognizable to anybody who's had her in seventh grade. "What did you pick?"

This question actually requires an answer. "Corn and beans." I shrug. "And"—I pause to swallow—"chickens and goats."

"Cool," he says.

"The Puritans gave Massasoit chicken broth when he was sick, so that's my proof for . . . chickens."

He nods.

"I thought about llamas, to herd the goats," I add to fill the silence. "But they didn't have them there. Yet, I mean." Then for some reason I add, "They spit."

I think Drew actually draws back when I say that. Or maybe he just has to get to class. Either way, he points down the hall, says, "Math." And he's gone.

I head for English, wobbly and confused, my heart going at record speed. Why did he stop to talk to me? And, "They spit"? Really?

Then an arm slips through mine. But it doesn't feel like it does when Cassie and I link arms, squishy and cozy. This arm is bony and bossy. And its owner isn't happy.

"Ms. Channing. Room five. After school," says Monica. She keeps a grip on my arm and walks me past my English class, making it look like we're old friends. But her voice isn't friendly. At all. "You know, Shira?" she says. "I tried being nice. I even took the time to show you how to pull yourself out of the social ditch you're in. I was even considering recommending hair product. And instead of being grateful? You stab me in the back."

"It wasn't my fault, Monica. Dr. Leeds wanted to do the scene, and just now—"

She drops my arm and looks at me. "Listen," she says. "It's not like Drew is going to look twice at somebody like you. So stop making a fool of yourself."

She puts two bright pink squares of gum in her mouth and repeats, "Ms. Channing. Room five. After school." Then she walks away, leaving the smell of Fruity-Berry Cherry Blast in her wake.

I hardly hear a word Ms. Corcoran says in English. I keep hearing Monica's voice, wondering what Ms. Channing needs me for. I doubt it's because the electric piano is broken again.

After school, I go to room 5. Ms. Channing is there, wearing a yellow suit, with a lapel pin of those tragedy/comedy theater masks. She sits in a classroom chair, her arm resting at a perfect right angle on the kidney-shaped fake wood writing desk.

"Shira, sweetie," she says, smiling, "have a seat." There's another chair opposite hers, and I squiggle in behind the desk. "You know that Monica and I both adore you." I guess I look skeptical, because she takes my hand and squeezes it hard with her long, dry fingers. "Truly, we do. We both appreciate your help so very, very much. You're an excellent understudy. And one with perfect pitch, too!"

I don't say anything. I just stare at the floor, where there's a puddle left over from some trombone player's spit valve.

Then Ms. Channing drops both her grip on my hand and her smile. It's like the "tragedy" half of her pin has taken over. "But I'm sure you've noticed, Monica is a bit bothered. She's the only one with an understudy, and it makes her feel less . . . capable."

"But—" I say. She holds up her hand.

"I know, I know. With her busy schedule, it was a necessary . . ." I'm bracing for the word "evil," but she catches herself in time to say, "decision. But now that showtime is approaching, Monica has assured me that she will be at every rehearsal."

I wonder if she's decided to learn her lines, too.

"So, I wanted to give you the freedom to . . . step away."

"Step away?"

"Yes, dear. Step away." Ms. Channing makes a sweeping motion with her hand, illustrating a graceful exit, like a ballerina twirling offstage.

"It's completely up to you, of course," she goes on. "But sometimes an artist's sensitivities require sacrifice. And I know you would do everything in your power to build Monica's confidence . . ."

Ms. Channing keeps going, but I'm not listening. It dawns on me that what Paul said is true. Monica is jealous. Of me. It's such an odd thought, that someone like Monica could be jealous of someone like me. But it also means that Monica wants me gone, and she'll make my life miserable until I am.

So I can dig in my heels, or I can make life easier for all of us. It seems like a simple choice. But my real problem isn't Monica. It's Marian. Stepping away from Monica is easy. Leaving Marian is what's holding me back.

Ms. Channing looks regretful—actually, she looks like an actress trying to *look* regretful.

"You know, Shira," she says, "I was thinking." She tilts her head in a way that signals she has something to sweeten the deal. "Mr. Hoover made the—somewhat odd—choice to cast you in the barbershop quartet. I know that Dylan would be happy to take that part. If you want to transition from that role, we can add you to the River City Ladies, or—"

"No!" I snap. Ms. Channing looks a little startled.

"Well, I just thought, if you'd rather be wearing a pretty dress than a hat and a mustache . . ."

"No," I say again. "I wouldn't." Then I manage to squeeze out "Thank you."

"Well, then." Ms. Channing folds her hands in front of her on the little half-desk. She's still waiting for my answer.

It's not like I have much of a choice. But as I'm about to answer, I realize it's not as hard as it first seemed. Because letting go of my role as understudy doesn't mean letting go of Marian. I'll never give her up. I'll still listen to her in my room. I'll still sing her songs. She's mine as much as she's anybody's.

So I look Ms. Channing in the eye and I say, "Of course. Whatever is best for the show."

"Well, all right then." The comedy half of the pin has seized back control, and Ms. Channing is all smiles again. She tilts her head and takes my hands in hers.

"You know, Show People don't dwell on disappointment. We keep our chins up and our eyes looking forward. One of my favorite sayings is, 'With every door that closes, another one opens.' I think it will be that way for you, Shira. I truly do."

With that, she walks to the door and swings it open for me, as if some great opportunity is waiting. But when I walk out, all I see are the gray, dented lockers and leaky water fountain that I pass every day. The door springs back and slams shut behind me.

Out in the hallway, I take a deep breath. Being understudy really didn't mean that much. It wasn't like I was going to play the part—I'd probably freeze up just like I had at the tech rehearsal, and it would be a total disaster. I remind myself how terrified I'd be if I had to actually play Marian. Imagining is one thing; doing it is another.

But still. Imagining is something. As long as I was understudy, I could fall asleep dreaming about being called in at the last minute, impressing everyone at school. Even Drew.

When I open the door to the music room for barbershop rehearsal, I'm staring at five faces: Cassie, Paul, Jason, Vijay, and Felix. I probably shouldn't have told Cassie about the meeting.

"What happened?" Cassie asks.

"I'm not going to be understudy anymore," I say in as matter-of-fact a way as I can.

"What?!" shrieks Cassie. "Why?"

"Monica's doing fine, and having me around made her feel less capable," I say, using Ms. Channing's word.

"She just doesn't want you standing in for her, because she knows you're better," says Cassie.

"So she just fired you?" says Jason.

"She didn't fire me," I say. "I resigned. Look, I didn't

exactly enjoy my quality time with Monica. And I wasn't going to play the part, anyway."

"An asteroid strike was still a possibility . . ." says Jason.

"We should talk to Mr. Hoover," says Vijay. "We'll tell him—"

I shake my head. "No, it was my choice. It wasn't fun anymore, with Monica glowering at me all the time. I don't want to be an understudy. I want to be Jacey Squires. With you guys."

"You know what?" declares Felix. "Monica's the one who loses. Now she doesn't have you to help her. She has to learn her lines on her own."

"And she's not going to, if she keeps leaving her score in the music room," says Vijay.

"So, you're okay then?" Cassie asks me.

"Yeah," I say. "As Ms. Channing says, 'When one door closes, another one opens.'"

"You believe that?" asks Vijay.

"Of course not," I say.

"Bummer for Paul," says Jason. "Now he can't even hope for that ki—" Vijay elbows Jason hard in the ribs. Paul is conveniently looking away, and I feel myself blushing a tropical sunset.

Chapter 27

Whomp, Whomp

The next day, Ms. Channing is late. I'm in the music room, waiting for her with the barbershop quartet and Paul, when suddenly the door bursts open and Monica charges in, followed by Melinda and Delilah. She's upset, or angry, or some combination of both. I wonder if some other piece from her makeup bag has gone missing. She looks around the room.

"Where is she?" she asks.

"Where's who?" asks Vijay.

"Ms. Channing. Isn't she here?"

"Not yet," answers Paul.

"Monica, what's the matt—" I start to say, but she just shoots me an angry glare. Even Melinda and Delilah are standing a few feet from Monica, like she's just too toxic to approach.

Monica is holding some messy strips of paper in her right hand. She looks around and drops them on top of the piano. I have no idea what they are. I watch her stand there, with her hands folded across her chest, wondering what she's expecting us to say.

"Well, you'll be happy to know I found my score," she says.

"I didn't know it was missing," says Paul.

We all take a few steps closer and look at the mess of paper. Now I can see that it's her score. Or had been. The pages have been cut horizontally into strips about an inch thick, and they're curled up like the fancy ribbon on a birthday present. The binding still holds it together, but just barely.

"Well, it *was!*" snaps Monica. "I left it there yesterday, on that chair"—she points to a chair in the front row—"and somebody took it, and . . . chopped it up."

"You left it yesterday?" asks Paul.

"Yes," replies Monica. "Or maybe the day before."

"So, you didn't even look for it for like two days?"

"That's not the point!" snaps Monica. "The point is, I just found it outside my locker. And it's been chopped."

Jason steps forward and looks at it closely. We all circle around, observing it from different angles. It's chopped, all right.

"Wow," says Jason. "Awesome."

"It's not awesome!" yells Monica.

"Not at all," echoes Melinda.

"Not at all," repeats Delilah, who has never been accused of originality.

Vijay bends his long body down and looks at the pages.

"Somebody had to use some major hardware on that," he says. "Regular scissors wouldn't go through all those pages so many times."

"It looks like it went through a bread slicer," says Jason.

"Or a pasta maker," adds Felix.

"Or maybe somebody used a hatchet," suggests Jason.

Vijay knits his eyebrows and stares harder, running his finger along one cut edge of the score. "No, I'd bet on a paper cutter. One of those big guillotine things."

"Yes!" says Jason. "Like the kind Mrs. Koch has in the art room."

"Oh, man, you could cut your hand off with one of those," says Felix.

"You're not kidding," says Paul. "I was down there just the other day. Mrs. Koch was using it. Felix is right. That thing is dangerous."

"You could slice right through muscle, cartilage, bone, you name it," Jason says. "*Whomp, whomp, whomp.* There'd be blood spurting halfway across the room—"

"Stop it," snarls Monica.

"I mean if you weren't paying attention . . . *whomp,* there goes your finger, bouncing onto the floor."

"Eww!" squeals Delilah, covering her ears.

"Wait," says Jason. "That's our clue. We can find out who did it for sure. Whoever's missing a hand, or a finger . . ."

I see Felix pulling his sleeve down over his fist just in time for Jason to grab his arm and hold it up with a dramatic "Aha!"

"You guys are gross," says Melinda, but Delilah looks almost like she's hiding a smile. Then something seems to occur to Monica. She turns on Paul.

"So you admit you were down there," she says.

"Down where? Admit what?" asks Paul.

"You were right there. In the art room. You admit you were there. You did this, didn't you! It's not enough that you have to declare your love on a locker—"

"What?!" Paul blats out.

"And upstage me all the time."

"I don't—"

"It's not fair. I'm the one with the title role," she states.

"The title role is the Music Man, Monica," says Vijay calmly. "*He's* the Music Ma—"

"Never mind!" yells Monica. "Anyway, you took my score, and when Mrs. Koch was finished with the paper cutter—"

"No, I didn't!" protests Paul. "And Mrs. Koch doesn't let kids get near that thing."

"Yeah," agrees Felix, "there's a big sign that says 'AUTHORIZED' . . . um, AUTHORIZED people or persons . . . something . . ." He shrugs.

"But somebody chopped my score," insists Monica. "And I know you were there."

"Paul wouldn't do that, Monica," I say. She looks at me, and I immediately regret opening my mouth.

"Oh, sure. There you go defending him again. You're probably in on it. I know it was you two who wrote on the locker. I've figured you out, Shira. You want to harass me so I'll quit. Then you take my part and learn every line with your perfect whatever-it's-called. And then you two can kiss on the bridge like you want to."

Why does everything always come back to me and Paul and that kiss?

Thankfully, Paul manages to ignore that last comment. He just says, "Nobody could have taken your score if you'd taken it with you, Monica. You were supposed to learn the 'Gary, Indiana' scene by today."

"Well, I couldn't exactly do that with my score gone, could I?"

Paul slaps his head and turns away.

"I think you're all in on it," says Monica. "Stealing my Jade and writing that horrible graffiti, and now this. You're all in on it. And I'm going to prove it."

Monica starts for the door, but then stops, turns back, and snatches the shredded score off the piano top. Then she stomps out into the hallway, chopped score in hand, with Melinda and Delilah marching dutifully behind her.

Chapter 28

Benched

"So, tell me again. How was it chopped? Like a salad?" We've been trying to describe it to Cassie ever since yesterday. Word has traveled around school, so now everybody knows about the mysterious chopper.

I'm hoping that Monica has calmed down and we can have a normal rehearsal today. Yesterday she worked alone with Ms. Channing. The rest of us drilled "Ya Got Trouble" with Paul. He was fantastic. Today, we're all heading for the music room, filling Cassie in on the details.

"Actually, it looked more like a bowl of pasta," Felix says. "The thick, flat kind."

"Linguini?" Cassie asks.

"More like fettuccini," says Jason.

"And nobody knows who did it?"

"It's one of those mysteries," I say. "The kind where there are so many people who have a motive it's hard to know where to start."

"Did you guys see *Phantom of the Opera*?" asks Jason.

"Mysterious things keep happening and it turns out there's this phantom haunting the opera house."

"You think there's a Phantom of the Middle School?" asks Cassie.

"I think so," says Felix, nodding. "Definitely."

"No," states Vijay, coming up behind us. "Somebody real is doing this."

"Yeah," says Jason, "but who? There's an army of thousands who want to get Monica back for something."

The music room door is halfway open, and we hear a voice coming from inside that I recognize as Melinda's. I hear her say something about the score and Paul. We stay hidden outside the doorway, listening to Melinda's story, trying not to make a sound.

"I was walking past the art room," she says, "and I saw Paul. He was chopping up Monica's score!"

There's a little mumble, I think from Mr. Hoover.

"Yes! Of course I'm sure. And I'm positive it was Monica's score."

"I was down there!" says Paul. "But I had social studies maps for Mrs. Van Der Watt. Mrs. Koch used the paper cutter. I never touched it!"

"Paul," says a man's voice. "I told you, buddy, you're on deck. Just sit tight." The voice belongs to Mr. Donnelly. He'd been Coach Donnelly, the school's athletic director, for about twenty years before he was promoted to principal.

"You're absolutely sure about this, Melinda?" asks Mr. Hoover. He doesn't sound at all convinced.

"Absolutely," says Melinda. Outside the door, we look at each other, not believing what we're hearing.

"Thank you, Melinda," says a soft-voiced Ms. Channing.

"And I just want to say that this collaborates the evidence on the locker." It's clearly Monica's voice. She must have spent all night memorizing a line like that. "Monica and Paul . . ." She makes a disgusted sound, like she can't even finish. "Who else but Paul would write that?"

"What?!" says Paul. "That's ridicu—"

"Or he had his girlfriend Shira do it."

I start to lunge for the doorway, but Cassie holds me back.

"Okay, so everybody calm down," says Mr. Donnelly. "Are you finished, girls? Okay, buddy, you're up." There's a slight pause.

"I already said I was in the art room, but I never touched Monica's score," explains Paul. "I was there for Mrs. Van Der Watt. Ask her."

"Well, Paul, the problem is, we did ask her, and she says she doesn't remember."

Vijay can't take it anymore. He jumps into the doorway

and says, "Mrs. Van Der Watt is like a hundred and two and she forgets everything. She thinks my name is Vincent."

Monica gasps dramatically. Next to me, Jason puts his head in his hands.

"Now, let's be respectful," says Mr. Donnelly. "And where did you come from, son?"

"I was outside," says Vijay, "and I'm a friend, a good friend of Paul's. And as his representative, I have some questions." Before anyone can object, he launches his questions. "Why didn't Melinda say something yesterday, if she saw Paul doing it? How did it conveniently take her till this morning to remember?"

"I, um, it's not that I didn't remember," says Melinda. "I was waiting to see if Paul would come forward and turn himself in." Monica had to have prepped her for that. I picture her nodding smugly, like an approving drama coach watching her prize student's performance.

"And if he did, I might have even accepted his apology," adds Monica.

"Oh, brother," mutters Jason.

"And why haven't you asked Mrs. Koch what happened?" continues Vijay, like a seasoned attorney.

"Mrs. Koch is at a conference, but we'll talk with her when she's available," answers Mr. Donnelly. "And—should he be here?"

"Vijay, why don't you wait outside," says Mr. Hoover.

"All right," says Vijay, "but Paul's telling the truth. The only way Melinda knows he was in the art room was because he said so." There's a slight pause, then Vijay says, "And by the way, Monica, it's corroborate. Not collaborate. And it doesn't corroborate anything." He comes back out to the hallway, and Cassie gives him a few congratulatory pats on the shoulder.

Inside, Mr. Donnelly continues. "Look, Paul, it's very possible that Melinda is somehow mistaken. We're going to look into this further. The problem is, meanwhile, we've got these practices for the play . . ."

"Rehearsals," says Mr. Hoover.

"Right. Rehearsals. And Ms. Channing has expressed to me that Monica feels . . ."

"Uncomfortable," says Ms. Channing.

"Yes, uncomfortable. And I can understand that she feels that way under the circumstances. So . . ." He pauses. I picture him putting a hand on Paul's shoulder. "Until we find out for sure who did this . . . well, I'll just come out and say it: I'm going to have to bench you for the next few practices."

"Rehearsals," says Ms. Channing.

"Bill!" Mr. Hoover protests. "Nobody's proven anything!"

"Now, that's true," says Mr. Donnelly, "and we're

going to find out more. But I'm not taking him out of the lineup . . . he's just sort of on injured reserved."

"But we're in the final weeks of rehearsal!" Mr. Hoover sounds really upset. "And Paul is by far the most important part of the show!"

"What?!" screeches Monica.

"Understood," says Mr. Donnelly. "But an accusation has been made, and we have to look into it. And the SPAM committee agrees that—"

"SPAM?!" shouts Mr. Hoover. "The SPAM committee has a say in this?"

"Let's remember, Tim, they've funded our guest director, as well as the bass drum you requested, and the jingle bells for that sleigh song. I love that song—"

"Are you serious?!" Mr. Hoover sounds like he might explode.

"Tim, let's calm down here," says Mr. Donnelly. "As I said, this is just temporary. And meanwhile, Paul, if you think of anybody who can confirm what you told us, you march him right into my office and I'll listen to every word. I'm not jumping to conclusions here. We're just . . . taking a time-out."

We don't hear anything else, except the squish of Paul's sneakered footsteps coming toward us. As soon as he hits the hallway, we surround him and hustle him down the hall.

"We heard everything," says Jason.

"We'll quit," says Vijay. "We'll tell them we won't be in the play without you."

"But why would she blame Paul?" asks Felix. "Without Paul, there's no show."

"I think I get it," says Vijay. "She saw an opening, when Paul said he was in the art room. So she accuses him, takes him down a peg, then she'll graciously forgive him and save the play."

"But what if she doesn't?" I ask.

"She has to. She wants to do the show, and there's nobody else who can play Harold Hill."

I don't even bring up what Monica said, about wishing Drew could be her leading man. And how jealous she looked when Paul sang "Seventy-Six Trombones." Could she really want to replace Paul with Drew? Even Monica couldn't be that self-centered.

Who am I fooling? Of course she could.

"Look, we'll call her bluff," says Vijay. "We'll just quit in protest."

"Vijay's right," adds Cassie. "They can't do the play without us . . . well, without me they can. But not without you guys."

"No! You can't!" Paul's stare moves from one of us to the next. "You can't put the play in jeopardy. I'm not out. I'm just—"

"Benched," says Felix.

"Sidelined," says Cassie.

"Designated hitter," says Jason. Felix shakes his head.

"I wouldn't be surprised if Monica did this herself," says Cassie. "Just to get attention."

"I doubt it. She looked pretty mad," says Vijay. "But there's got to be a way to figure out who did it."

"We don't have to," I say. "We just have to prove that Paul didn't."

"Hey, Shira's right," says Felix. "It doesn't really matter who did it. We just have to prove that Paul is innocent."

"Right," I say. But I have no idea how.

Kids are pushing past us, going into rehearsal.

"So, what do we do?" asks Jason.

"Go to rehearsal," says Paul.

"Without you? No way." Jason shakes his head.

I feel the same way, but I know how much the show means to Paul. "No, Paul's right," I say. "We'll figure this out, but for now, we keep the show moving ahead. And besides, if we don't, Monica's just going to gloat. Tomorrow we'll figure out how to clear Paul."

Everyone's looking at me. "What?" I say.

"We're waiting," says Jason. "For the plan."

I look at Cassie, then at Vijay. But they both look stumped.

"Okay," I say. "There's that student government assembly tomorrow."

"Ugh," moans Jason.

"No, that's good for us," I say. "We'll get there early, sit in the back row. Everybody, think over all the possibilities. We can compare notes tomorrow, and come up with a plan."

Rehearsal is about to start. Kids are passing us, heading to the music room.

"Shira's right," says Paul. "We'll meet tomorrow. Now go to rehearsal. I'll be fine."

We all watch as Paul quietly walks away, like a star quarterback forced to leave the field. He turns back and smiles at us like nothing's bothering him at all. And that's when I know just how good an actor he really is.

We go inside and Mr. Hoover calls me over. "Shira," he says, "what's this about not having you as understudy anymore? Ms. Channing says you changed your mind."

My stomach jumps. I don't want Mr. Hoover to think I quit. But things are already so topsy-turvy, I don't want him worrying about me. Not when Paul is depending on us to get him back in the show.

"Yeah, I—we had a discussion. Ms. Channing and me."

"A discussion. I see." Mr. Hoover scratches his chin.

I nod, trying to look confident. "So, Monica is doing fine on her own, and she has no more auditions—"

"In The City," Mr. Hoover adds with a half-smile.

"In The City," I repeat. "And she needs her confidence, and I . . . I really couldn't handle it all," I lie. Mr. Hoover doesn't look convinced. "Really, I just want to be Jacey Squires." And right now, that's the truth.

Mr. Hoover finally nods. I think he understands everything, especially the fact that right now we're both thinking about Paul.

"We're going to get Paul back in, right?" I ask.

"Of course we will," he answers. But I wish at least one of us sounded like we believed it.

Meanwhile, as Mr. Donnelly chats with Ms. Channing, Monica's forces are lining up opposite Felix, Jason, and Vijay.

"So, you heard the news?" Monica says to Felix. "Paul did it."

"He did not," says Felix. "You're making it up."

"Melinda saw," says Monica, "and now he's out of the show."

"He isn't out of the show," says Jason. "He'll be back."

Mr. Donnelly comes over, making a T-sign with his hands. "Time-out now. Nothing's final yet. Let's all calm down and let the dust settle. We'll be reviewing the call before we make any final ruling. Ms. Channing?" She turns to Mr. Donnelly. "Can you run some plays without him?"

"Numbers," Mr. Hoover grumbles, at the same time as Ms. Channing says, "Scenes."

"Good," he says.

The room is filling up. I see Monica take Drew by the arm and sit him down next to her, telling him everything. Soon everybody knows all the details and the room is buzzing.

"Show People! Show People!" Ms. Channing calls over the noise. "We have a play to put on." She claps her hands, but it seems like no one is listening. "Kids!" she tries, and when that doesn't work, she switches into a new gear.

"LADIES AND GENTLEMEN!!" she bellows. Her voice comes from somewhere down deep in her chest.

It's quiet. "Ladies and gentlemen," she repeats, "I know we're all a little distracted by . . . things . . ." She waves all that away with her hand, and I can't help feeling that it includes Paul. "But it's rehearsal time. Now, let's get started." She consults her clipboard. "Everyone, to the auditorium, we need to rehearse . . . oh dear." She looks over to Mr. Hoover. "We were going to work on 'Ya Got Trouble.'"

"Ya Got Trouble" is one of Paul's big numbers.

Mr. Hoover nods, like he's seen this coming. "We can rehearse the townspeople," he says, "so they'll be ready when Paul gets back."

For a second, I feel better, hearing him say that Paul will be back.

"And I can go over 'Will I Ever Tell You?' with Marian

and the barbershop quartet," offers Ms. Channing. "We're all here, aren't we?"

"That's the one where I sing the melody and they do the backup stuff behind me, right?" says Monica.

Not exactly. Marian sings "Will I Ever Tell You," while we sing "Lida Rose." They're equal parts, written to fit together.

But of course, to Monica, it's her number. And of course, she knows that the last thing we want to do just now is harmonize with her.

Still, we don't have a choice. We follow Ms. Channing to room 5 and Monica sings about how she'll never tell Harold Hill that she loves him, even though she does, and we sing our love for "Lida Rose" like we've done a million times. Except, for us, something's changed. We're not being led by Mr. Hoover anymore. We're not watching Ms. Channing. We're watching each other. We're hearing each other and we're bonded together like we've never been before. We know our notes, and we know one another's notes, and the harmonies sound tighter than they've ever sounded.

And after we're done, we walk away from Monica like everything's fine, because the last thing we want is to clue her in to our plan.

If only we had one.

Chapter 29

The Blue Marauder

The next day, we all meet up as planned. The assembly is being held in a room called the LGI. Nobody knows what LGI stands for—but it's a tradition to guess, and the theories range from "Large Gastro Intestine" to "Land and Gorilla Institute." It's basically an auditorium with desks set up for big lectures and test taking. For some reason, the chairs are attached to the desks with these swiveling metal bars, resulting in a sort of mini version of the Whip ride in an amusement park. I don't know what they were thinking.

Anyway, it takes some concentration to anchor ourselves, but we try to stay focused. We don't have a lot of time. Five kids are running for student government president. We've raced over so we have time to hatch our plan before Kevin "I'll-go-first" Clancy takes the stage.

"So, listen," says Jason. "Dylan said he's going to sing Harold Hill's part in rehearsal."

"And how bad would he be?" asks Cassie.

"Let's put it this way. He sang Hansel in third grade,

and I was rooting for the witch. If he has to sing 'Ya Got Trouble,' I'll just jump out the window."

"Look," I say, "we don't have a lot of time. We have to prove that Monica and Melinda are lying—"

"Which they are," adds Jason.

"Or prove that Paul is telling the truth," says Felix.

"Which he is," says Cassie.

"Do you have an alibi?" asks Jason.

"Not really," says Paul. "I mean, I was in the art room, but I didn't have Monica's score."

"He shouldn't need an alibi," I say. "They have no evidence. Just Melinda's story."

"But Donnelly's going along with it," Cassie says.

"Well, he made a bad call," says Jason.

"He's off base," says Vijay.

"He didn't even see the tag—" Cassie adds.

"Stop joking around," says Felix, giving Jason a push that sends him traveling into Vijay and Vijay into a stranger on his right.

After they right themselves, Cassie says, "Seriously. We've got to do something."

"Do you think—" starts Felix, who's interrupted by Mrs. Highsmith, who's here to monitor the assembly. She's a chunky lady who wears sensible shoes and the same army-green pantsuit every day.

"Too much noise in here!" she calls out. "We'll be

starting in—" She looks over at Kevin, who taps the microphone with no response. "We'll be starting shortly!"

We're quiet for about thirty seconds, then Felix continues, this time in a slightly shaky whisper, keeping one eye on Mrs. Highsmith. "Do you think whoever really did it might give himself up? Do you think . . . he should?"

I've been so wrapped up in figuring out how to prove that Paul didn't do it, I haven't really given much thought to figuring out who did. I look around, and it occurs to me that the mystery chopper could even be one of us. Vijay's so smart. He could've easily planned it all out. And behind the goofy exterior, I know Jason hates the way Monica bosses everybody around. Cassie resents Monica. Maybe she took matters into her own hands. Felix? Maybe he's had enough of following the rules.

"If he turned himself in, he'd be in big trouble," Jason says.

"Or she," adds Cassie.

"I'd hate to see somebody get in trouble." Paul looks a little sad at the thought. "It was just a joke."

"And it's not like Monica didn't deserve it," Vijay says. "If you leave your score lying around like that."

"Really, it was pretty creative." Cassie smiles. "It's kind of like we have our own masked hero."

"Or heroine," I add.

"A Phantom," Vijay says.

"The Teen Avenger," says Felix.

"The Blue Marauder," says Jason.

"What's a marauder?" asks Felix.

"I'm not sure. But I think it has something to do with pirates, or looting," says Jason.

"Why blue?" I ask.

"I don't know. School color?"

"Our school color's green," says Felix.

"I hate green," says Jason.

"Look," says Paul, pulling us back to the matter at hand, "I'm sure he, or she, never intended for me to get the blame. I say we give it twenty-four hours to prove I'm innocent, then we put out a plea for the chopper to come forward, to save the show."

We all nod agreement.

"Have you talked to Mrs. Van Der Watt again?" Cassie asks Paul.

"She doesn't remember a thing. I think she thinks my name is Steven."

"How about Mrs. Koch," I suggest. "Is she back?"

"I don't know. Anyway, Monica will just say I did it behind her back."

"Still, she can verify that you were in the art room for Mrs. Van Der Watt's project," says Vijay. "And maybe she knows who else has been there. We need to talk to her."

"I'll go after school," says Paul.

But Cassie's shaking her head. "We shouldn't wait. She might not be there after school. Why not now?"

"We're here now." Jason looks grim. "And nobody leaves when Mrs. Highsmith is in charge." We all look up front at Mrs. Highsmith. She stands straight, arms folded, scanning the crowd for trouble. Dr. Leeds is fiddling with the microphone. We hear it chirp and then blast some ear-shattering feedback.

"Nobody's allowed to leave? Wanna bet?" Cassie is a firm believer that rules are optional. I think it has something to do with her parents getting divorced. It somehow compromised her belief in authority.

"Leave it to me," she says, and she walks up to the front of the room, where Mrs. Highsmith is standing. We all start traveling nervously in our sliding chairs.

"She's crazy," says Jason.

"She'll never do it," adds Felix.

"I don't know." Vijay shakes his head slowly. "Don't be so sure."

We watch Cassie as she starts talking to Mrs. Highsmith.

"Look," says Vijay. "Look at that. She's listening."

Sure enough, as Cassie speaks, Mrs. Highsmith cocks her head a little to the left. Then she looks up at our group, nods, shakes her head like "Isn't that a shame," and then she makes a motion with her hand like, go, go. Cassie comes back and says softly, "Okay, Shira, let's go."

"Wow!" Vijay is clearly impressed.

"How did you do that?" asks Felix.

"Shh," she says, glancing back at Mrs. Highsmith. "I just told her Shira and I needed to leave. Don't make a big deal out of it."

Paul is already halfway out of his chair. "But why only Shira? What about me? I'm the one who's in Mr. Donnelly's penalty box."

"Yeah, no fair," adds Jason.

"If you have to know," Cassie says in a whisper, "I told her that Shira . . . needs to go to the girls' room, for female reasons, and she's too embarrassed to ask for herself." I think I actually open my mouth to scream, but Cassie shuts me up with a look. "She gave me permission to go with her. If you want to come along, I'm going to have a lot more explaining to do."

I must be about a raspberry sorbet color by now, but the looks on the boys' faces also make me want to laugh. If there's one thing that makes a boy speechless, it's mentioning female stuff. I've never seen them all clam up so fast. Cassie grabs me by the hand.

"Hold your side or something," she says, and we hurry downstairs, to the art room and Mrs. Koch.

Chapter 30

The Jaws of a Crocodile

The art room is on the basement floor of the school, so we scamper down the stairs, hoping that Mrs. Koch will be there. I like Mrs. Koch. She has short white hair and wears dangly earrings, with special ones on holidays. On Halloween she has flashing pumpkins and at Christmastime last year a sleigh and reindeer.

Cassie and I arrive at the art room and we're relieved to see that the door is open. We walk in and look around the room. It's empty, but as we're about to turn around, we hear a clunk coming from the supply closet.

"Hello? Mrs. Koch?" calls Cassie.

"Over here!" Mrs. Koch's head pokes out of the closet, up at a height of about eight feet. We can't see the rest of her, but there's something about the look on her face that tells us she could use a hand. We make our way over to find her up on a step stool, trying to keep a pile of multicolored paper from tumbling down from the top shelf with one hand, while hanging on to a huge plastic jar of paint with the other. Cassie moves faster than I do, grabbing the paint and freeing Mrs. Koch's hand to catch the pile of paper.

"Almost got me that time," she says, climbing down from the stool. "One day, someone will find me done in by an avalanche of Cray-Pas." She takes the paint from Cassie and thumps it down on the table, then she smiles a friendly buck-toothed smile, shakes her earrings, and says, "Anyway, what brings you down here?"

We tell her about the show, about Paul and Mr. Donnelly, Monica's chopped score and Melinda's accusation, and how we hope that maybe she'd seen something that would clear up the confusion.

"And who was the girl who said she saw him?" she asks.

"Melinda Croce," I answer.

Mrs. Koch's eyes narrow a little. "Her mother's the chair of SPAM, right?" We nod. Somehow, I don't get the feeling she's a big fan. "So, she says she saw Paul at the paper cutter with the score."

"But he says he was just bringing some maps down here for Mrs. Van Der Watt—"

"But Melinda says he waited until you weren't looking, and he chopped the score," I finish.

"Well, maybe I'm absent-minded, but I would never leave a student access to that paper cutter. You could cut your hand off."

Cassie and I both nod. Mrs. Koch stops to think for a few seconds.

"How thick is the score?" she asks. I hold up my fingers to show her—about an inch, even an inch and a half. "This isn't a great paper cutter. It would take a long time for someone to chop up something that thick. This was what, about three days ago?"

We nod. She thinks for another minute. "I do remember Paul was here. And I trimmed the maps. It only took a second. I really doubt that he would have been able to chop something like that without me noticing." Cassie and I smile. "But I don't know if that's enough to change anybody's mind." End of smiles. "Now, if he'd used the one upstairs, it would've been much easier."

"The one upstairs?" I ask.

"In the guidance office. I'd like to have one like it down here, but then you get into school politics, budget cuts, cozying up to the parent committees. In fact, I requested one from the SPAM committee, but they used the money for a bass drum and some bells for that Christmas song . . ."

"'Sleigh Ride'?" offers Cassie. There are those jingle bells again.

"Yes, that's the one. I remember the meeting. They looked right through me like I wasn't there. Reminded me of high school." I'm getting the feeling that when mean girls grow up, they join the SPAM committee.

"Anyway," she says, "the paper cutter in the guidance department could cut something like that easily. It would only take a minute."

Cassie and I look at each other, and then Mrs. Koch gets the same idea.

"Let's go," says Cassie.

Walking through the halls with a teacher is a special feeling. The hall monitors let us go right by, like we're suddenly promoted to being trusted. I wonder if that's what it's like to grow up. We come to the guidance office, and Mrs. Koch takes us into a little room where there's a copying machine the size of a rhinoceros, chugging away and spitting sheets of paper out, about five per second. Just behind it is another paper cutter, and this one is twice the size of Mrs. Koch's.

"Look at this," she says, with a little shake of her head. "I guard mine like a hawk, and this one is completely unattended." She gives a little *tsk*, then lifts the blade by its handle, like she's prying open the jaws of a crocodile. I take a step back from the big metal blade, but Mrs. Koch bravely looks down into the slot where the blade comes to rest, then gently lowers it again. She looks at the cutting surface, then pokes her head behind it, around, and under.

"By the way," she says. "Did the score have a cover?"

"An orange one," I say. "It was chopped, too."

She switches a little latch that locks the arm down, then

tilts the entire cutter back. And there, underneath, are dozens of little clippings, white, with orange ones mixed in, barely thicker than threads and as long as the width of a piece of paper. Or the width of a music score.

"Voilà," says Mrs. Koch. "Your evidence."

Chapter 31

Mistaken

We leave Cassie there in the guidance office to guard the paper cutter and the little scraps of paper. Mr. Donnelly's office is on the other side of the building, and we don't want to risk having someone tamper with it. I'm not sure what Cassie will do if somebody wants to use the paper cutter, but I have faith in her.

As we leave the guidance office, the bell rings. Everybody comes pouring out into the halls, happy to be free, even if just for four minutes. Mrs. Koch is amazingly good at maneuvering through the student cross-streams. She leads the way, moving fast, and I stay right behind her.

I have a class starting in three minutes, but I don't care. This is too important.

We go by the LGI and see Paul and Jason leaving the assembly. Vijay and Felix are right behind them. I wave them over and they push their way through the crowd.

"We're going to Donnelly's office," I call over the noise.

"Donnelly's office?" says Felix. He looks worried.

"We're not in trouble. We found white and orange

clippings in the guidance office paper cutter. The guidance office!"

"So, whoever did it, they did it in there, not in the art room," says Vijay, getting it right away.

"And Melinda's story goes south!" says Jason.

"You're geniuses!" says Paul, all his enthusiasm returned.

"If you're coming, let's go," says Mrs. Koch. "I'll write you late passes for next period."

"Yes!" said Jason. Felix still looks reluctant.

"Wait," says Vijay. "Where's Cassie?"

"Back in the guidance office," I say. "Guarding the evidence."

He drops off the pace a little.

"Are you coming?" I ask him.

"Cassie might need backup," answers Vijay. He skips a few steps backward and points over his shoulder. "You go to the office. I'll go wait with Cassie."

"And I have a science test," says Felix, looking at Donnelly's door like it's the gate to Azkaban. "You go and explain. I'll catch up with you later."

"He really needs to chill," says Jason, watching Felix go. The bell rings for seventh period. Jason goes into Donnelly's office and I'm about to follow, but out of habit, or self-destruction, I glance down the hall, toward Drew's locker.

He's there, with Monica. Her back is toward us, but I can tell she's chattering away. I know I have to go. The last thing we want is for Monica to see us all trooping into Donnelly's office, but my eyes lock on Drew. He opens his locker and a soccer ball bounces out. He jogs after it, and as he bends to scoop it up, he sees me. He raises a hand, and my breath stops somewhere between my lungs and throat.

"Shira," says Paul. "Come on." I raise a hand back, then quickly, before Monica can turn around, I duck into Mr. Donnelly's office.

There are two desks inside, but both assistants are out. Mrs. Koch looks at the clock, then she motions for us to follow her and knocks on Mr. Donnelly's door.

"Deb?" says a voice that sounds far away.

"No, it's Nancy Koch," she replies loudly. "I have some kids here who need to see you, and they have to get to class." No answer. "Bill? Can you hear me? It's important."

"Yes . . . I'm just . . . Come in . . ." calls the voice, this time sounding sort of pinched. Mrs. Koch motions for us to follow as she opens the door.

Mr. Donnelly is in his suit pants, shirt, and tie, on the floor, on all fours, with his left arm stretched out in front of him and his right leg stretched out straight in back. His tie hangs down ninety degrees to the floor. He stays frozen that way for about ten seconds, then switches—right arm, left leg, and says in a strangled voice, "Have a seat . . . exercises for my back . . . last one." He's making a conscious effort to breathe evenly, but the word "one" barely makes it out. Mrs. Koch casts a quick glance our way, then looks at the ceiling, sighs, and motions us to a couple of chairs by Mr. Donnelly's desk. After about twenty seconds, he stands up and starts to touch his toes.

"Bill," says Mrs. Koch in a stern voice. "Take a break. These kids have class." Mr. Donnelly stands up, brushes the lint off of his shirt, and returns to his principal self. He straightens his tie and sits on the front of his desk.

"So, what's the crisis?"

"Bill, there's been a mix-up about that music score." Mr. Donnelly looks a little blank, so Mrs. Koch says, "The one that was chopped up." That seems to jog his memory. "Evidently, Melinda Croce was quite sure that Paul used the paper cutter in my room to destroy it."

Mr. Donnelly looks over at Paul and says, "We benched you, right, son? From the play?"

"Uh, that's right," says Paul.

"Well, these kids came to me," Mrs. Koch continues, "very responsibly, to see if that was possible, or if I'd seen anyone else using the paper cutter."

"Good," says Mr. Donnelly.

"I realized that the score was too thick for my paper

cutter, so we went up to the guidance office, where they have one that is far superior to mine. And far less supervised," she adds, with a low-grade glower. "And there are clippings. White and orange. They're clearly from the score. Whoever cut up the girl's score—"

"Monica," says Jason, and both Mr. Donnelly and Mrs. Koch look at him like they hadn't noticed he was there. "The girl is Monica."

"Thank you," says Mrs. Koch. "Whoever cut up Monica's score didn't do it with my paper cutter. They did it in the guidance office." Mr. Donnelly looks confused again and Mrs. Koch goes on very slowly and deliberately. "So, Melinda has to have been mistaken. She might have seen Paul in my room, but he wasn't cutting up Monica's score."

"So, there's no evidence against Paul," I say. "It had to have been somebody else."

Jason looks at me and mouths the words "The Blue Marauder."

"Well," says Mr. Donnelly, "let me talk to Mr. Hoover and Ms. . . . uh . . . Ms. . . . ."

"Channing?" I suggest.

"Yes. It does sound as if Melinda could have been mistaken."

I would have said lying, but I'll settle for mistaken if it means that Paul is cleared.

"So, Paul's back in!" Jason declares.

"Well, we'll have to gather the team and discuss it. I'll let you know as soon as I can."

"But—" I start, but Mrs. Koch places a hand softly on my shoulder.

"Why don't I take you down to see the evidence," she says to Mr. Donnelly. "There's a student there waiting for us." I can't believe I almost forgot about Cassie. "Meanwhile, these kids have to get to class." She turns around, and we follow her out to Mr. Donnelly's assistants' desks. She locates a late pass pad and fills them out for us.

"Bill!" she shouts into his office. "Come on. It'll only take a second." Then she whispers, "Say thank you," and we join in a chorus of, "Thank you, Mr. Donnelly!"

"You're welcome, kids. All right. Lead the way, Nancy. I'll take a look and see if we can get this kid back on the field."

"You'll be back in," Jason tells Paul. "You're cleared. It's obvious."

"I hope so," Paul answers.

"See you at rehearsal," I say, and I nod, "for sure."

Chapter 32

The Most Unassuming People

By seventh period, the entire school knows every detail of the story, down to Melinda's Oscar-winning performance yesterday and Mrs. Koch's heroic hallway march today.

But when I hurry into the music room with Vijay and Jason after school, Mr. Hoover tells us to be patient. Mr. Donnelly is talking with Ms. Channing right now. He tries to sound confident, but I can tell from the way he's doodling on the piano that he's nervous. He's playing "Goodnight, My Someone," but it's hidden inside all sorts of complicated, dusky chords. It makes me picture him slouched over a piano in a smoky jazz club in some black-and-white movie.

The three of us sit down and listen to Mr. Hoover's improvisations.

"I'm worried about Paul," I whisper.

"I know," says Vijay.

"But they have to let him off," I say. "We proved it, right?"

Vijay nods.

"You think we'll ever find the real Blue Marauder?" whispers Jason.

"I doubt it," says Vijay. "He's probably gone into hiding."

"Or she," I add, because Cassie isn't here, and I know that's what she'd say.

"Maybe we should set a trap," says Jason. "Hide a video cam in the piano. See if anyone tiptoes in in the dark of night."

"We could get someone to go undercover. Hire a mole." Vijay shifts his eyes back and forth suspiciously.

Mr. Hoover switches to a rendition of "Shipoopi," a favorite song with the seventh- and eighth-grade boys, because anything that sounds like "poop" will be a favorite with seventh- and eighth-grade boys.

"Hey," says Jason, "have you ever thought . . . maybe Mr. Hoover is the Blue Marauder?"

"Mr. Hoover?" says Vijay. "That's crazy."

"Maybe he's trying to scare Ms. Channing away," says Jason. "It wouldn't take much to send her over the edge."

"Oh, come on," says Vijay. "Look at him." Mr. Hoover is wearing his lavender polo shirt, khaki pants, and loafers.

"I can't really see him chopping a score or writing stuff on a locker," I add.

"Unless he wanted to throw you off his trail. Make it look like a kid did it," says Jason.

When Felix arrives, Vijay asks him. "You don't think Mr. Hoover is the Blue Marauder, do you?"

"Whose stupid theory is that?" says Felix. Vijay looks at Jason.

"We were just talking . . ." says Jason. "I mean, sometimes it's the most unassuming people who have something to hide."

"Hmmm . . . then maybe it's Felix," says Vijay.

"Me?" Felix looks terrified.

"Seriously, Felix? You're like the last person I'd suspect," says Vijay.

Felix looks relieved, but a little disappointed, too.

Vijay is watching Mr. Hoover. "I wonder if he really wanted to be a rock star. Or a jazz pianist."

"Maybe he still does," I suggest. We're all thinking this over, when Mr. Hoover looks up and sees the four of us examining him like he's a stuffed mountain lion at the Natural History Museum. We all smile innocently.

"No. No way," Vijay mutters. "I would admit that I was the Blue Marauder before I would say it was him, and I know it's not me, so there's no way it's him."

Before I can even think that through, the River City Ladies come in, led by Delilah, who plays Mrs. Shinn. And rehearsal begins.

On the schedule is "Pick-a-Little, Talk-a-Little," and our song, "Goodnight, Ladies." They're written to fit together, so as we're singing the smooth "Goodnight, Ladies," they're chirping and gossiping and spreading rumors. A lot of the gossip is about Marian.

Mr. Hoover starts with their part. They race through their tongue-twister lyrics, catching breaths whenever they can and spewing out gossip. I think about that day after I found out about my perfect pitch. The whispering, the giggling. That's what the River City Ladies do to Marian. That's what people have always done, I guess. And I bet it always hurts.

The barbershop quartet slides into their chatter with "Goodnight, Ladies." We answer their gossip with a smooth goodnight. They can cackle all they want. Today, I'm with the gentlemen. Not that it's easy to hold on to our melody with all their picking and talking going on. It takes a lot of concentration, and when we reach the end of the song, we're all exhausted. Mr. Hoover plays the last chord with a flourish.

And Paul is standing in the doorway.

"Hey, Mr. Hoover?" Paul says. "Can you come to room five? Ms. Channing wants your help with 'Shipoopi.'"

"'Shipoopi'?" says Felix. "Wait! You're back in the show?"

"Back in the lineup," says Paul, with a grin.

"Yes!" cries Vijay, and even the River City Ladies give a cheer. Jason whacks Paul on the arm, Felix and Vijay are high-fiving, and before I even realize what I'm doing, before I can even remember to be shy, or unsure, or embarrassed, I charge at Paul, and then I'm squeezing him around the middle in a giant hug.

It's just a few seconds' hug. A congratulations hug. A hug that I break off before anyone thinks it's any other kind of hug. Because it's not. It isn't at all.

Mr. Hoover grabs Paul's hand for a handshake and a "Welcome back!" Then he pats him on the shoulder, and the two of them go off to room 5 for "Shipoopi."

We have the afternoon off, and I practically skip to my locker. I can't believe it. Paul is cleared.

Felix is already at his locker, three down from mine. He's spinning his combination lock, and dancing in place, singing a line from "Shipoopi."

"We did it!" I say.

"I can't believe it!" says Felix.

"It was the best feeling, when we—"

But just then I see something fall out of Felix's locker. It rolls a couple of feet across the floor toward me. It looks like a colored pencil, but it isn't. It's a blue-green color, and on its side in fancy letters it says "Jade." Felix snatches it up, but it's too late.

"Felix," I say, staring at the eyeliner in his hand.

"That's . . ." I look around, making sure nobody else is there. I lower my voice. "Is that Monica's Marimba Teal eyeliner?" He nods. "Did you know it was there?" He nods again, his brow furrowed.

"Have you had it all along?"

"I didn't take it. I found it. It must have fallen out of her bag. I didn't even know it was hers, at first."

"But did you . . . were you the one who wrote on the . . ."

He looks down. "Yeah. I knew she'd hate that."

"Was that all?" He keeps looking down and shakes his head. "Felix," I say, swallowing hard, "did you . . . chop the score, too?" Now he looks up at me and I can see the answer in his face.

"Felix!" I say, much too loudly. I look around and see we're still alone, but even so, I go back to a whisper. "Felix. You . . ."

"Monica was so mean, to you, and to Cassie, and to Paul, too. She kept leaving her score in the music room, like she didn't even care. It was just sitting there that day, all curled up. I took it, and then I was walking by the guidance office and I saw the paper cutter there with nobody around. I didn't plan it. It was just so easy. One more day and I would've turned myself in. Really."

I keep staring at him. It doesn't compute. Felix, the Blue Marauder.

"Please don't tell anyone," he says. "Everything's fine

now, right? I don't want to get in trouble. They'll suspend me, or worse, they'll take me out of the barbershop quartet, and it's like the best thing . . . the best thing I've ever done."

I look at his panicked face. I don't know what to say. I've never been asked to keep a secret like this. But how could I tell on him? He's right, there's no way they'd let him sing in the barbershop quartet.

"I won't tell," I say, although I think Jason and Vijay might have new respect for Felix if they knew. "Just, no more, okay?" I add, I guess to make myself feel less guilty.

"Okay," says Felix. "But . . ."

"What?"

"There might be one more thing. It's sort of . . . already in progress. It doesn't hurt anybody or anything though. I promise."

I take a deep breath. "Okay," I say. "But no more after."

"Deal," says Felix. He zips the Jade safely inside his backpack and hoists it onto his back. "I promise. Thanks, Shira. You're the best."

"Sure. See you tomorrow," I say, and then I whisper, "Blue Marauder."

Chapter 33

Purple Garlic

It takes all my willpower not to tell Cassie. We've never kept secrets, but I've made a promise.

It helps that everyone's attention is on Paul. At the next "Seventy-Six Trombones" rehearsal, he gets a cheer before he even starts. Mr. Hoover ordered Monica a new score, and with the show coming up fast, she doesn't have time to devise any other revenge plans, though if she did, the new suspect would probably be me.

It seems like Ms. Felt has finally gotten Monica working on her lines, because she's using the script less and less. Maybe she finally realized that learning "by heart" and memorizing are kind of the same thing.

Somehow Paul manages to rehearse his scenes with Monica as if nothing happened, but all Paul ever wanted was for the show to go on, and he's getting his wish.

With the show barely two weeks away, a last-minute panic is starting to set in. Every day there's something else that reminds us that showtime is just around the corner, and maybe the biggest of those things happens today.

I'm on my way to English when I hear kids starting to talk about it. I hear it from Cassie, who heard it from Vijay, who heard Delilah telling Melinda how she'd seen the men unloading two big boxes from an orange truck.

The costumes have arrived.

It's like the Wells Fargo Wagon scene, with the wagon arriving and everyone getting excited. Not that kids are exactly singing in the hallways, but you can hear everybody squealing and talking. Teachers are threatening detention if we don't calm down and pay attention for another two periods. When the final bell rings, we all run down to the music room.

Inside, girls are jumping up and down and giggling. The boys are trying to look like they don't care, but they've raced down here, too, so everybody knows they're excited. The two huge cardboard boxes have "Travel Wardrobe" written on their sides. Each one is nearly six feet tall, and Mr. Hoover is standing next to one of them with a screw-driver in his hand, staring menacingly at the box as if he's waiting for it to make the first move. Ms. Channing looks for directions, craning her neck around the back of one of the boxes like some exotic bird.

Monica stands next to her, an annoyed look on her face. "It must say 'Open Here' somewhere," she says. "We're just not looking in the right place."

Kids are offering their own suggestions.

"Just rip it open!"

"Blow it up!"

"Call the janitor."

Finally, Dylan waves his clipboard and says, "Everybody, sit down. Let Mr. Hoover figure it out."

Monica sits in the first row, obviously wanting to be there first when the boxes are finally opened. I sit in the third row on the other side. After I sit down, I see that Drew is in the same row. He has one foot up on the chair in front of him. I count the empty seats between us. Six. I try not to look at him, but my eyes won't listen. They dart over to see that he's holding a bunch of wrinkled pages that look like they've been trampled by a herd of muddy elephants, with diagrams and arrows. I think they must be soccer plays.

I wish I could say something witty, maybe about soccer plays or elephant herds. Anything but spitting llamas. But I know it would all get caught in some maze of twists and turns between my brain and my mouth. And even though she's focused on the costume boxes, I know Monica would somehow hear me. And most of all, what's blocking my brain-mouth passage is the memory of him standing so close, his hand on my shoulder, and that almost kiss.

I hear someone yell out, "Go for it, Mr. H!" and Mr. Hoover takes a stab at one of the staples on the box's side. He digs at it for about a minute, but each staple is four inches long and made of some industrial brass that looks like it's shrugged off hammers and crowbars ten times the size of Mr. Hoover's screwdriver.

Monica heaves a dramatic sigh, then turns around and slaps the knee of the boy behind her. She points to Drew, who's still looking at his elephant-trampled papers, and the boy gets the point. He gives Drew a "Hey, dude," pointing to Monica.

"Drew, sit here," she says, reaching back practically into that same kid's face to grab Drew's hand and pull him to the front. Drew mumbles a little "sorry, man" as his soccer pages knock the second-row kids in the head. The chairs make sad little groans as their rubber feet scrape the floor.

"Embarrassing," Cassie whispers to me, and I think at first she's talking about the trampled kids in the second row, but I realize that she means the defeat Mr. Hoover has suffered due to those giant staples. They glare at him, shiny and intact.

Quietly, Vijay walks up beside Mr. Hoover. He whispers something and Mr. Hoover gives Vijay the screwdriver. Vijay studies the box, then very gently pries two big tabs out of their slots. Then he pulls, and it opens, like a magic closet—without a rip or a tear.

There's a cheer, and a few "Vijay" calls. Vijay takes a little bow, and then he comes to sit next to Felix, who gives him a victorious fist bump.

A few kids start to get up, but Ms. Channing stands in

front of the wardrobe, her arms out and slightly behind her, like she's protecting her children from an advancing mob.

"Stop!" she calls out. "I will call character names and you may come up *in an orderly way*. Make sure you have the correct size and *hand them back* to Mr. Hoover. I repeat. Hand them back. Costumes do not go home!" She calls out the first one. "Zaneeta Shinn!" Melinda stands, and after making sure that her sweatpants waistband is folded perfectly just below the waist, she goes up to grab the deep red skirt and ruffled blouse from Ms. Channing's hand. She holds it up in front of her and spins around.

Ms. Channing takes out the next skirt and calls, "Alma Hix!" Amanda Delios creeps up to gently take her skirt, which has yellow and green checks and is about twice the width of Melinda's. She doesn't flounce at all. In fact, she practically crawls back to her seat.

Cassie goes up when Townsperson Number Eleven is called and collects her skirt and blouse—both sort of a dirty beige color, and she shoots Ms. Channing a look before returning to her seat.

The barbershop quartet is called, and we're handed our matching blazers. But when we hold them up, instead of ugly, they look sort of dapper.

Ms. Channing calls Eulalie MacKecknie Shinn, and Delilah collects her costume. I guess Monica has waited long enough. She gets up and stands beside the second wardrobe. "Mine must be in here," she says. "Can we just open this already?"

Ms. Channing gives an almost imperceptible sigh and calls out "T.J.!" Vijay stands and slowly makes his way to the second wardrobe. He opens it up easily. Monica pulls out the band uniforms that fill half the box and practically throws them to Melinda, who hands them off to Mr. Hoover.

Meanwhile, Monica has found her dresses. She pulls them out and goes to a corner where she can admire her new wardrobe. Her first outfit is modest, a pretty pink-and-white dress: Marian, the piano teacher.

Cassie shoves me with her elbow. "You would make such a better Marian," she says.

Monica's second outfit is for the Marian the Librarian scene, when she has to look especially bookworm-y. It's a black skirt and white blouse with a little black bow tie. Monica tosses that one aside, digging through the costumes for her last dress—the party dress for the final scenes. Its skirt is a mass of ruffles, and it's wrapped in plastic and a thin layer of tissue paper. She rips it open.

Then she freezes.

It's purple. It has tulips and bulbs.

"Purple! No . . ." She starts softly, but gains momentum, moaning, "No! I ordered blue! I ordered the BLUE one! With the flowers, not the onions!!"

By now, everyone's attention is on Monica, and it's not just a couple of kids who are holding in giggles.

"And look at it! It's huge. It's like ten sizes too big!"

Then she drops it to the ground and turns to Ms. Channing. "Ms. Channing, it's horrible! It's an ENORMOUS PURPLE DRESS WITH STUPID, STUPID GARLIC!!

Ms. Channing tries to calm her down, but it's no use.

"I'm not going to wear this. I would never wear this. NEVER!!!! You have to order me a new dress. Someone made a stupid, stupid mistake!"

I try not to look at Felix, but I can't help it. I shoot him a glance and his eyes meet mine. And that's when I know that the Blue Marauder has struck again.

Chapter 34

Murray

Ms. Channing must have some connections, because the very next day an overnight package arrives with Monica's petite-sized blue-flowered party dress. But even with that crisis overcome, getting so close to showtime is making everybody twitchy. It's so bad in science that Mrs. Franklin threatens to cancel our next experiment, where she'd promised flames and smoke.

Ms. Channing is showing signs of the strain. Her hair pins are starting to slip. The cheery tone is fast becoming history.

We have our first run-through, which is known in show business as a "stagger-through," for reasons that soon become obvious. We survive, but kids are still forgetting lines and missing entrances, exiting groups crash into entering groups, and half the set is missing for "Seventy-Six Trombones." In "Wells Fargo," all the kids sing their solo lines on cue, but the first time Cassie sings her "Or a double boiler," it gets caught in her throat after "dub," and when Ms. Channing runs the number again, Cassie screeches it out, but the top note lands a little low and the last note sails way too high.

A few kids laugh, and I see Cassie cast a quick glance over at Monica, whose mouth is crunched up in a little self-satisfied smile.

When I get to today's rehearsal, Felix and Jason are busy trading watches, to see whose watchband smells the worst. Sean Battaglia is lobbing cheese puffs at random targets. Ms. Channing is preparing to give us our notes on yesterday's run-through.

Cassie sits down next to me and says, "I think you should sing my line. You're standing two people away, just sing it and nobody will know."

"Cassie," I say, "you'll be fine. Just practice a little at home and—"

"I've sung it like five hundred times! My mother is about to ship me off to my dad's permanently. I can't do it. Everybody's going to laugh at me."

"They're supposed to laugh!" I say. "Don't let Monica—"

"But she's right. I'm just not a good singer. If I can't get the notes, I can't get people to laugh, except *at* me."

"You can," I say. "You'll get it." But after yesterday, I have to admit, I'm wondering what it will take.

Ms. Channing is trying to get our attention. It would help if Mr. Hoover were here, but he's trying to sort out where the missing half of the set has gone.

"Now, please," Ms. Channing calls out. "Ladies and gentlemen, please! It's time to buckle down." A few kids shush the others, but there's still an undercurrent of nervous giggles and comments.

"I have notes for everyone," she calls out. "Some are specific, some are general, so I need everyone to listen to everything. First of all, everybody must project to the very last row!" She turns to Sean, just as he launches a cheese puff at Vijay. "Sean, you're going to have to tone down Winthrop's lisp. It's a lisp, not a rain shower." That gets the boys laughing, but Ms. Channing continues. "Drew, we need a little more energy from you. Remember, you're Tommy Djilas, the bad boy in town." A few eighth-grade boys shove Drew on the shoulder, repeating "bad boy" about a hundred times. He ducks a little and shakes his head. "Next, remember, stage right is *on your right* as you stand *on the stage, looking at the audience*. And I cannot stress enough how important it is that—"

Then she stops. In mid-sentence. It's like in a nature show, when the gazelle freezes, hearing a stampede coming her way. She seems to be listening to something none of us can hear. And we get quiet, too. Somehow, Ms. Channing's stillness works in a way that all her attempts to get our attention didn't. All the fidgeting stops and we listen.

We can hear footsteps, but they're very faint, coming from down the hall—a slow *squish, squish* of rubber soles and another set, more of a hurried *scuff, scuff*. They get louder and louder, until finally, a man I've never seen before appears in the doorway, and then behind him, Mr. Donnelly.

"Ms. Channing," Mr. Donnelly says. "Sorry to interrupt practice, but this gentleman said it was important." Then he lowers his voice, but we can still hear him perfectly well. "I would have called and had you come to the office, but my secretary left early, and I'm not all that handy with the phone system. So, I brought him down here. Is it a bad time?"

He looks around the room at all of us staring wide-eyed at this new visitor. I'd say it's a bad time.

Ms. Channing's eyes are fixed on the visitor, too. He's about five foot two and bald. He wears a black ribbed shirt that clings tightly to his shoulders, as well as to the potbelly that sits just above his belt. A gold chain hangs around his neck, with a matching one around his wrist. I think I see Ms. Channing's chin quiver, and she seems to need to summon some strength just to say one word.

"Murray."

"Hayley," the man says, reaching a hand toward her. Even though he's about fifteen feet from her, she pulls back, turning away, her glance fixed on the fire escape window, where a poster of a bear with a fire hat says "This Way to Safety."

We're all quiet. We don't have a clue what's going on, but

we know that if we make a sound we might never find out. For a minute it's like they've forgotten we're here—a room full of twelve- and thirteen-year-olds—not an easy crowd to forget.

"Ms. Channing," whispers Mr. Donnelly. "If there's a problem—"

"No," she replies, lifting her chin higher. "There's no problem. He's . . ." She pauses and swallows and says, ". . . an old friend." If I didn't know what a "dusky voice" sounded like before, I do now.

"Maybe you should . . ." Mr. Donnelly motions to the hall with an over-the-shoulder jerk of his thumb. Ms. Channing nods and steps out into the hallway with Murray. "Now, kids," Mr. Donnelly says, "I'm expecting you to wait quietly for a few minutes. Just go back to what you were doing, and Ms. Channing will be right back."

The thing is, we weren't really doing anything, so there isn't anything we can get back to. And even if we were, there's not a chance in a million that we'd get back to it, with something this exciting happening in the hall. So, as soon as the door clicks shut, we rush to the doorway to listen.

"Shhhh-shhhhh," says the kid closest to the door. "I think I hear something."

Then Melinda calls out, "They're back here!" She's standing by the double doors in the back of the music room, the ones that lead to the rear of the auditorium stage. Ms. Channing has taken Murray there, where she thinks they'll be alone.

Melinda is looking through the crack where the doors meet, and soon we're all crowded around behind her. Monica pushes to the front.

"Shhhh-shhhh. He's talking," whispers Melinda. "It's something about a show." She listens with her ear to the crack. "It never opened," she says quickly, to fill us in. "The out-of-town critics killed it." There are a few murmurs, but Melinda shushes us again. "He says she was right. He was chasing a playpen . . . no, wait. A daydream. He says he was chasing a daydream. A ridiculous daydream."

"Poor Murray," I hear Cassie whisper.

"Now he's—it sounds like he wants her to go with him. Somewhere, I can't hear what . . ."

"Let me try. Monica pushes Melinda out of the way. She kneels down on the brown and beige floor tiles and presses her ear to the crack.

"He's talking about *Chicago*," whispers Monica. "In Springboro."

"I thought Chicago was in Illinois," says Jason.

"Not the *place* Chicago, the *show Chicago*," snaps Monica. "He's begging her to say yes."

"Say yes, my dahling," I hear Vijay whisper.

"What's her answer?" asks Jason.

"I don't know. I don't hear anything," says Monica.

"Are they still there?" asks Cassie.

"I think they're kissing!" cries Melinda, who's standing

behind Monica and peeking through the crack. That starts Sean and his friends making gagging noises. I try my hardest not to picture the scene in too much detail.

"Now what's happening?" asks Cassie.

"I don't know. I think they're gone."

"Who's gone?" It's Mr. Hoover. He's come in from the hallway and is standing there, staring at us. Nobody really wants to be the one to answer. Finally, Dylan breaks the silence.

"Um . . ." he says, pointing. "Ms. Channing and a little bald man."

Mr. Hoover looks at us quizzically. "When I get back," he says, his hand on the doorknob, "I want to see you all in your seats. Sitting quietly."

The door closes and about a hundred conversations start at once.

"So, is she going to Chicago?" asks Felix.

"How many times do I have to tell you," says Monica. "It's the *musical Chicago*."

"In Springboro." Melinda nods.

"Where's Springboro?" asks Paul.

"I'll tell you one thing. It's not Broadway," mutters Cassie.

"It doesn't matter where Springboro is," says Melinda. "Don't you know a big break when you see one?"

"It was just like in the movies." Delilah looks dreamy.

"My mother told me she was getting over a big split," says Monica. "With a major director."

"And that's him?" Jason doesn't sound at all convinced.

"Please," says Monica. "Can't you tell by looking at him?"

I didn't want to say anything, but no, I couldn't.

"So that's why she was crying all the time," says Melinda.

"It was just one time," I say.

When the door starts to open, we rush back to our seats and hold our breath. But it's just Mr. Hoover again. He looks around suspiciously. We look like little models of good behavior.

"So," he says, in a take-charge kind of way, "it seems that Ms. Channing has something to tell you." We all look to the doorway, and Ms. Channing makes her entrance. She looks slightly rumpled, her makeup smudged a little, but she carries herself more erect than ever. She picks up a shawl that she'd left on a chair and throws it around her with a flourish.

"Ladies and gentlemen," she says. "Sometimes, when you least expect it, opportunity flies down like an angel and lands softly on your shoulder." I look over at Murray, who is gazing at her adoringly from just outside the doorway. "That angel can find us any time, any place. Even here!" Her arm flies out and she seems to be pointing to a blackboard that says in big letters "TEST WEDNESDAY."

"And when that opportunity alights . . ."

I look at Murray again. He's trying to sneak a peek at his watch.

"We have no choice. And although my heart breaks to leave you, my talented, beautiful players, I'm afraid . . . I must." No one says anything, but she holds out her hand, as if she's holding off a mass protest. "No, truly, I must. I'll remember all of you darling boys and girls, and I wish you a brilliant, beautiful, breathtaking performance. Break a leg, everyone, break a leg!"

Then she puts both hands to her mouth, blows us a kiss, and goes to the door, where Murray is waiting. She takes his hand, and they leave.

Even though we heard it for ourselves, it's hard to believe she's gone.

Mr. Hoover still stands by the doorway. He looks from the door to the piano and starts to reach for the phone.

"Call to the bullpen," whispers Vijay.

But Mr. Hoover doesn't pick up the receiver. Instead, he turns to us, claps his hands together, and says, "Okay, guys. We've got a show to put on. Ms. Channing was right."

"About something, anyway," whispers Cassie.

"We've got three days to pull this together, and we have to get moving to make this work." He pauses for a second and looks at us. "*You* have to make this work." He picks up Ms. Channing's chart, glances at it, then puts it down. "Townspeople, let's go over every one of the general chorus numbers, including 'Ya Got Trouble' and the 'Seventy-Six Trombones' finale. The rest of you, we'll go with the schedule. Those of you scheduled to work with Ms. Channing, Ms. Pappalardo will take her place. Go over the scenes you're the *least* confident about. I'm trusting you to be serious about this. Okay, everyone, let's get to work."

I'm surprised at the excitement I feel seeing Mr. Hoover up there. I'm still more surprised that everybody seems to feel the same way. I think we all realize that he's right. If this show is going to happen it will be because of us. Not Ms. Channing, not Mr. Hoover, but us.

Kids scurry around, heading for their rehearsal rooms to go over their scenes. Drew goes with Melinda, and the others leave in twos and threes. Monica and Paul head for the doorway, but before she goes, Monica turns around.

"I hope you all realize that we're now part of musical theater history," she declares. "I say, let's put on the best show ever. For Ms. Channing."

We all pretty much ignore her and turn our attention to Mr. Hoover, who sits down at the piano and starts the introduction to "Iowa Stubborn." And oddly enough, I think maybe Ms. Channing was right about something else, too. Maybe when one door closes, another one does open. Because for the first time since Ms. Channing came to Hedgebrook, I feel like *The Music Man* belongs to us.

Chapter 35

Showtime

"Do you have to throw up?" asks Sophie. "I heard that lots of stars throw up before they go on stage."

"I'm not a star," I say, not admitting that throwing up had crossed my mind.

It's hard to believe, but the night of the show is here.

I've tried not to think about it. I've avoided our refrigerator, where on the calendar, Saturday is marked in red, "7:30 P.M. *The Music Man.*" At school, there are posters all over, with pictures of trombones blasting out "Fall Musical! *The Music Man!*" and every time I passed one this week, my stomach did a flip-flop.

I keep reminding myself that I'm ready. Over the past three days, Mr. Hoover recruited Mrs. Koch to help get the sets finished, and Mrs. Highsmith to drill everyone on their lines. He got us permission to skip study halls and meet in the auditorium or in an empty classroom, or even in a corner of the hallway, to go over anything that needed work. Mrs. Koch has had the crew hammering and painting from 3:00 until 6:00 every afternoon. The cast has gone home at 6:00, and then we've come back to work some more from 7:00 until "as long as it takes," as Mr. Hoover put it, sometimes until 10:00 at night.

We wore our costumes for dress rehearsal and sweated and squinted under the lights, and pushed through every mistake and missed entrance and wrong note. We've run our numbers so many times, I've even been rehearsing in my sleep. Sophie told me that she heard me singing something about bells and roses at 3 A.M., and I woke up one morning half out of bed, sure that I was making my entrance for "Goodnight, Ladies."

But tonight is different. Tonight we report for makeup at 5:30, and there's an audience watching, and there's no next time.

Mr. Hoover has given us our last-minute reminders: No perfume. No waving to our friends in the audience. No flip-flops, no gum chewing, and no high heels.

I know I'm ready. But what if I open my mouth and nothing comes out? What if my knees shake and I can't even stand up? What if I look out into the audience filled with kids and parents and grandparents and freeze?

Nobody's advice seems quite right. My parents' catch-all advice when I'm feeling insecure is "Be yourself." It always sounds so logical and easy. But what if you think you know yourself, and then you find out that that's not all there is to you? What if there's this other person you find peeking out

from behind a curtain, and even though it's you, it's someone you hardly know? Maybe that's what I've really been
afraid of. Not being up on stage in front of an audience,
but finding out that I like it.

I stand in our front hallway, ready to go, dressed in my
khaki pants and white shirt. My plaid jacket, my straw hat,
my bow tie, and my mustache are waiting for me at school.
I've packed a bag with a pair of jeans and a T-shirt to change
into after the show.

Could there be an after the show? It seems incredible
to me that after all the work, everything we've put in, there
could even be an "after."

"What do they say in show business?" says my father.
"Break a leg?"

"Yeah, I guess."

"That's stupid," says Sophie.

"Well, I'll say it anyway," says my father. "Break a leg,
Shira."

"Can we come backstage when it's over?" asks Sophie.

"There isn't a real backstage," I answer. "It's just the
music room."

"That's okay," says Sophie. "We'll come there."

"Are you sure you don't want a ride?" my mother asks.

"I'm sure," I say. I want to walk. My grandmother used
to say that sometimes she just needed to hear the sound of
her own footsteps. Now I think I know what she meant.

My mother has been holding herself together admirably, but she finally bursts into tears and a "Good luck, sweetie. I'm so proud of you," and gives me a hug. My father comes over and takes his turn. I breathe in the smell of his aftershave and lean into the crinkly softness of his shirt and let myself feel like a little girl just for a second. Then I head off, on my own, and walk through the quiet autumn evening to Hedgebrook Middle School. After all, I know the way by heart.

It's just like rehearsal, I try to tell myself, but opening the music room door is enough to tell me that it isn't the same at all. Facing me is a jumble of kids getting made up, putting on costumes, everyone's nerves jangling. Lights and mirrors glare around the room, making the air hot and thick with the chalky, sweet smell of pancake makeup.

Kids are having their faces smeared with foundation as they flinch and squirm. Then comes lipstick, age lines, and all colors of eye shadow. It's amazing and eerie and exciting all at once.

Our makeup director is Johnny Haber. He's the best artist in school and he's recruited a crew of makeup helpers, which was an easy job. If there's one thing that isn't hard to find at Hedgebrook, it's girls who are into makeup.

I find Jason, Felix, and Vijay clustered together.

"Do we have to?" asks Jason.

"I think so," says Felix.

"Does it hurt?"

"Just your manly pride," says Vijay.

When it's our turn, we sit down in a row. Johnny makes a beeline to help Laura, my makeup artist, with the task of turning me into an ornery blacksmith named Jacey Squires.

"First," he says, pointing to my mass of curls, "we have to get that in there." He holds up the straw hat, then pulls out a box of bobby pins. The two of them start pinching and holding and pinning, wrestling my hair into submission. Laura tugs and Johnny pins, and I try not to flinch as my head screams for mercy.

Next to me, I hear Jason talking to his makeup artist. "I have naturally rosy cheeks," he says. "My mother always says so."

Through my bobby-pin haze, I look across the room, where in a corner, away from the chaos of the rest of the room, I can see Monica. Melinda Croce's mother is doing her makeup, with Melinda and Delilah watching. I guess SPAM moms do makeup, too.

Melinda has some pretty pink ribbons in her hair and her face glows with rouge. She's really taken to playing Zaneeta, Tommy's girlfriend, especially since Drew took over the role. In fact, in rehearsal, when Monica wasn't watching, I'd see a secretive smile creep onto Melinda's face.

I have to admit that Delilah looks alarmingly like an old lady as Mrs. Shinn, the mayor's wife. Her hair is sprayed with white, and dark wrinkle lines are painted on her forehead. With Philip Sussex, who's playing Mayor Shinn, she looks ready for Sunshine Senior Living.

Johnny and Laura finally manage to get my hair stashed away under my straw hat, and then Laura starts on my makeup. It doesn't take long. No mascara, no lipstick, just some eyebrow pencil and a few character lines. I wonder if I should look in a mirror or leave it to the imagination.

I breathe in the smell of all that makeup, somehow knowing that it's a smell that will always bring me back here, to this day and this place.

Cassie comes over to watch as we all get our finishing touches. She's wearing her beige dress, but she's added a sash and an old-fashioned hat with a bright red fake flower on it. Her makeup artist has given her a pretty blue shade of eye shadow and red lipstick that matches the flower. But she doesn't look happy.

"Cassie," I say, "you look fantastic."

"I can't do it," she says, ignoring my comment completely. "All I can think about is my one line, and how I'm going to mess it up. I've got this creaky voice, and I sing off-key."

"That's the point," I say. "You're a River City lady who's excited about the Wells Fargo Wagon. You're not a singer, you're just somebody who everybody in River City loves, despite—" I stop and correct myself. "Who everybody loves because of her creaky, off-key voice."

Vijay and Paul have wandered over, and I'm hoping they can give me some backup.

Cassie is shaking her head. "But everybody's just going to laugh at me."

"So, prove Monica right," says Paul. Not exactly the kind of backup I was looking for. "Show her you have the perfect voice for that line. Get the biggest laugh. You've got the best line in the whole show!"

"It would be easier if I had perfect pitch," says Cassie.

"It's not about perfect, Cassie," I say.

"Shira's right," says Vijay. "You're going to outshine everybody with your creaky voice. Because that's who you are."

"I'm creaky?" says Cassie.

"Um, no," sputters Vijay. "I mean, you're special. You're not like anybody else. And you're funny, and you're fun, and you're amazing. And you look beautiful."

Even through all the makeup, I can see that Cassie is blushing.

"You're going to nail it, Cass," I say. "You are." Cassie's blush is catching, and between the bobby pins squeezing my head and the straw hat and the makeup lamps all around, I'm already feeling like a rotisserie chicken.

"Now, I think we need to get dressed," says Vijay. It's time. We put on our matching plaid jackets, and then Jason and Felix come over. They put on their straw hats to match mine.

Over Cassie's shoulder, I see Monica. Her eyeliner and mascara are perfect, her hair is styled and shining. She looks ready for a magazine cover. Like a star. Drew is over there with her, and Monica playfully adjusts his suspenders, holding on to them for a few seconds and smiling up at him.

Paul has gone to get the rest of his costume. He comes back over, wearing a suit and a straw hat like ours, and carrying a small suitcase that says "Professor Harold Hill" on the side. He takes off the hat and bows to me.

"Harold Hill, at your service," he says, and I have to smile. I can't help remembering how he'd introduced himself that first day, skidding on the floor, when I didn't know a thing about him.

Vijay pulls his bow tie out of his inside jacket pocket. Mine is sitting on a chair, and I pick it up. Felix and Jason start to attach theirs, but Vijay looks at the funny clasp on the back of his, puzzled.

"Here," says Cassie to Vijay, "I'll do it," and she starts to attach it to his collar, right under his Adam's apple, which jumps once and then settles down. I fumble with my bow tie for a few seconds, until Paul holds out his hand and I place the little tie in his palm. He starts clipping the tie to my collar, adjusting it gently.

I can't help thinking, I've spent twelve and a half years without a boy's face this close to mine. And then there was Drew, up there on the bridge. And there was that hug with Paul, and now here he is, his fingers brushing my chin, his nose inches from mine. I notice how he knits his eyebrows and bites his lip a little, concentrating. His face is covered in makeup and his eyelashes look especially dark brown and thick. He looks older than the first time we met, that day that seems so long ago. Maybe he hit one of those teenage growth spurts, or maybe it's that I know him now. He only looks up into my eyes once, and we both look right down again.

"There," Cassie tells Vijay. "Just right."

"You too," says Paul.

Felix and Jason come over. We have our hats, we have our bow ties. There's just one thing left. And we want to do it together.

"One, two, three," says Vijay, and we take out our mustaches and stick them on, all at the same time. They're light brown and curled at the ends, like the mustaches kids paint on pictures. Our makeup artists hold up hand mirrors so we can see. We all start to laugh, but not for long, because the stick-on glue pulls on our lips and it hurts like crazy.

Mr. Hoover comes in and claps his hands. "Okay, quiet everyone. Quiet! Let's go over a couple of things before we start." We all crowd around him to listen. Everyone is so nervous that we all forget about normal middle school behavior, which is to ignore the teacher. Instead, it's perfectly quiet. I think even Mr. Hoover is surprised.

"Now, this is it, folks." I wonder if everybody has the same jolt of panic as I do. "Just a few reminders. I know the makeup feels weird. But don't rub your eyes or scratch your face." I look at Felix, whose nose instantly begins to twitch. "Well, try, anyway," adds Mr. Hoover. "And gum," he says with a sigh. "If you're chewing gum, take it out, please." Lots of jaws stop moving, and a few kids slink over to the wastepaper basket in the corner.

"Now," he goes on, "everybody, take a deep breath. Remember all the hard work you've put in. Remember how good you can be." Then he smiles. "Just have a great time out there. You're going to be terrific." He casts a glance over at Cassie and adds, "All of you." Then he says, "Okay . . . places, everyone!"

It's showtime.

Chapter 36

Sincere

"Are you nervous? I'm nervous," says Jason.

"I think I just choked on my own spit," says Felix.

"I don't think I have any spit," says Jason. "Does anybody have any water?"

"Guys," I say, trying to convince myself along with them, "we're going to be fine."

"Come on, our cue is coming up," says Vijay.

We've been out on stage for "Iowa Stubborn" and "Ya Got Trouble" and "Seventy-Six Trombones." But now it's time for the barbershop quartet's first number.

So far it's been incredible. When Paul started "Ya Got Trouble," you could almost hear the audience's amazement at all of those words pouring out of his mouth. Monica sang a pretty good "Goodnight, My Someone" with Amaryllis, and Melinda and Drew made a pretty convincing young-and-in-love-but-her-father-doesn't-approve couple. But even though Drew did all his dance steps right and he didn't flub any lines, he never seemed to relax completely. He never looked like he did out on the soccer field. Or even at the Bar Mitzvah. He never looked like he was meant to be there.

Not like Paul does. I remember what he said, about not doing the right things, in school, at recess. But when he sings "Seventy-Six Trombones," it's like all that energy and enthusiasm finally finds its place. Paul fits in. More than that. He's exactly right.

But now it's time for our first barbershop song. This is where Mayor Shinn enlists us to get Professor Hill's credentials. First, we'll sing "Ice Cream," then we'll go into "Sincere." I stand there waiting, sandwiched between Felix and Jason. And then I hear our cue, and I don't know which one of us pulls the others, but suddenly we're all out on stage, right up front.

The lights are bright, and I can hardly see the audience. I look at Jason and at Felix, and they say their lines, and then I look ahead, and there's Paul. He looks so confident, like he's enjoying every second. He's Harold Hill, and I am Jacey Squires. And I have a job to do. I say my line, and that's when I can finally relax, just a little, just enough. There's something in the way Paul looks at me that tells me it will be okay.

Paul gets us singing "Ice Cream," and then he blows his pitch pipe and starts us out,

How can there be . . .

And we take it from there.

. . . any sin in "sincere" . . .

Where is the good in "goodbye"?

I stand between Felix and Jason, and we follow Mr. Hoover's direction to drape our arms over one another's shoulders. My hand rests on Felix's bony back on one side, and Jason's chubby shoulder on the other. And we sing, each on our own part, but together.

Yes, my knees are shaking. Yes, it's different with an auditorium filled with people and the spotlight on and everyone watching. But as we get to the second line, and I listen to the harmonies take shape, I realize that we sound good. It's just like Mr. Hoover said. We've become a unit. We're a sweaty unit, a funny-looking unit, a hodgepodge of shapes and sizes, highs and lows. And maybe this isn't the cast of characters I would have ever imagined as my friends, but that's what they are. I'm exactly who I want to be, exactly where I'm supposed to be. In my dapper plaid jacket, with my hair stuffed in my hat and my mustache stuck fast on my upper lip.

When we get to the end of the song, I think I see Mr. Hoover wink. Maybe it's one of the spotlights reflecting off his piano lamp, but I don't think so. I think he's saying "I told you so."

When we get to "Goodnight, Ladies" and "Pick-a-Little,

Talk-a-Little," the audience wants an encore. Mr. Hoover nods to us and we make our entrances all over again and sing it through one more time.

And Paul is fantastic. Backstage, everyone keeps slapping him on the back and giving him high fives. Monica only forgets her lines twice, and Mrs. Highsmith is right there prompting her, so I doubt the audience could even tell.

Everyone is scurrying around, taking their places for "Wells Fargo." I've been so busy with the show, I've forgotten all about Cassie. I look over to the spot where she's supposed to be standing, and she's not there.

My mind jumps to the worst-case scenario—she's just too nervous, she won't be there to sing her line. I don't want to sing it for her. It's Cassie's line and she should sing it her way.

But just as I'm about to grab Vijay by the arm and ask him to go find her, I see her. She's added two more bright fake flowers to her hat. She holds out her arms, as if to say "Here goes. This is me. Take it or leave it."

I smile and mouth across the stage, "Nail it."

And the music starts.

O-ho the Wells Fargo Wagon is a-comin' down the street,
Oh please let it be for me!

The knee bounces and shoulder-wags and skirt-flouncing are more energetic than ever. In fact, everybody's so enthusiastic that we start speeding up the tempo, and Mr. Hoover has to take one hand off the piano and motion for us to take it easy. The first verse flies by, and Terry sings about his maple sugar, Rashawn wonders about his mackinaw, Nicole marvels about her grapefruit from Tampa, and we're on to the second verse. Cassie's bouncing along with everyone, and as her line gets nearer, I see it all in her face—fear, determination, and finally, a kind of freedom. Edward sings, "*It could be curtains,*" and Gianni follows with, "*Or dishes.*" Then Cassie comes in, belting out, "*Or a double boiler!*" in the loudest, creakiest, funniest, most full of gusto voice anyone at Hedgehog has ever heard.

Half the cast breaks into applause, and the audience erupts in laughter that can probably be heard on Broad-WAY. And the rest of us keep singing, with Cassie loudest of all:

Or it could be somethin' special
Just for me!

Chapter 37

Break a Leg

At intermission, we pour into the bathrooms and back into the music room. Everyone's jitters have been replaced with excitement and waves of exhaustion. My bobby pins are starting to loosen, and my straw hat tilts to the right, but my mustache is holding, and my bow tie is still in place.

The first thing I do is hug Cassie. "You did it!" I say.

"I did, didn't I?" she answers.

A lot of the girls are having their makeup touched up, and the boys who play kids are pulling their socks back up to look like knickers. In one corner, I see Monica sitting on Drew's lap. She's combing his hair, giggling at the way they've slicked it back to play Tommy Djilas.

"He looks great," says Cassie. I nod. "Too bad she's all over him like hot fudge on a sundae." I shrug and try not to care, adjusting my hair-stuffed straw hat.

It seems like we hardly have time to get a drink of water before Mr. Hoover announces "Places!" for the start of Act II.

Act II starts with the River City Ladies doing a ballet. Mrs. Shinn takes it really seriously, but it's actually a lot of middle-aged Iowans doing funny poses to the poem "Ode on a Grecian Urn." Then Harold Hill and Marcellus do "Shipoopi," and the ladies do "Pick-a-Little, Talk-a-Little" again, without us this time. And then it's our turn for "Lida Rose."

I remember the first time we sang "Lida Rose." How it all fell apart. How I couldn't imagine it ever sounding right. I remember that day when we had to sing it with Monica's "Will I Ever Tell You?," the day that Paul was banished.

But tonight, when Monica comes in with her part, I'm not thinking about her. I'm thinking about Marian. How up until now, she's spent her life imagining her "someone." And even now, when she's falling in love with Harold Hill, she'll only tell him so in her dreams. I'm glad Marian comes around in the end. And I'm glad I'm in the barbershop quartet, singing our love songs out loud.

When we've finished "Lida Rose," I can hear my mother cheering for me louder than everybody. I look across the stage, where a sign above the barn reads "Jacey Squires, Blacksmith," and I smile. That's me. Jacey Squires. My name in lights.

When we walk offstage, I feel a wave of relief. "Lida Rose" was our last barbershop quartet number. We've done our job. I stand in the wings, surrounded by Jason, Vijay, and Felix, waiting for our next cue, when we mingle with the other townspeople at the ice cream social. We've sweated through pretty much every article of clothing, so now we're all just as soggy as Jason.

We watch a dance scene from the wings, and then it's time for Paul and Marian at the footbridge. Paul is onstage, by the bridge, waiting for Marian. Monica makes her entrance, brushing briskly by me. She's wearing the blue flowered dress, and as she scurries across the stage, her fancy heels click-clack on the floor. She pauses dramatically when she gets onstage.

"Just go already," Jason mutters, and I elbow him to be quiet.

"Give her a break," says Vijay. "Poor Marian the Librarian. She's"—he holds the back of his hand to his forehead and bats his eyelashes—"conflicted."

"Apprehensive," says Cassie, who has come up behind us.

"Overcome with doubt," Felix adds.

Onstage, Harold Hill sees Marian and flashes a charming smile.

"Paul's good," says Jason. "You really wouldn't know that he hates her guts."

Monica takes an exaggerated breath and starts for the bridge. Paul really does look happy to see her. She rushes up to the bridge and Paul takes a step toward her. They're on opposite sides, a spotlight on each of them, just as I'd rehearsed it that day with Drew.

"You're late," says Paul, and despite our careful choreography, Monica takes three quick steps up onto the bridge. The spotlight swerves to follow her, and it finds her just as her leg does this funny bend, and then buckles, sending her down on the footbridge with a crash and a shriek. It sounds like a cat, or an angry blue jay—but it isn't either one. It's Monica. She's lying on the bridge screaming "My foot! My foot!" Mr. Hoover stops playing and signals to Alex Howell, who is operating the curtain, and Alex starts pulling the rope as fast as he can.

The audience is buzzing, and I can make out a couple of voices saying, "What happened?"

"Is she all right?"

And one shrill voice calling, "Monica! *Monica!*" But the voices get muffled as Alex pulls harder and the curtain closes.

We all rush onto the stage and Mr. Hoover pushes his way through. No one wants to get too close, because Monica is still screaming, at Paul and at anybody who gets near her, but we all want to see what happened.

"It's stuck! My ankle, it's stuck," she screams. "One of you idiots do something! It's broken. I know it's broken." And then she's crying and screaming all at the same time. I creep near enough to see that the heel of her shoe is stuck in between the slats of the bridge, her foot is stuck in the shoe, and the rest of her is sort of facing the other way.

"Look," says Alex. "Her heel is caught."

"No wonder," says Jason. "Those heels are like a foot high."

"Who built this stupid bridge?" Monica yells. I guess in the heat of the moment, her admiration of Drew's handiwork has slipped her mind.

I spot Felix, whose forehead is now a torrent of wrinkles, his mouth open and his eyes glued to Monica's foot. I have an awful thought.

There's so much talking and screaming, there's probably not much risk of being overheard, but I pull him off to the side, just to be sure. "Felix!" I whisper-shout, afraid to ask. "Did the Blue Marauder—"

"No! No, I would never do anything to hurt anybody. It's her shoe. They said not to wear heels."

"So you didn't—"

"No, I promise!"

"Okay, I believe you," I say. "Really. I didn't think you did. The Blue Marauder is cooler than that. But I had to be sure."

Felix still looks stricken that I could've doubted him. But I pat him on the back, and we squeeze in between Jason and Vijay, just in time to see Monica's mother come crashing through the center opening of the curtain.

She rushes over to her daughter. "Monica! I'm here, Monica!"

Mr. Hoover has managed to get Monica's foot out of the shoe, which is still stuck in the slat of the bridge. Alex tries to tug it out, but it's like it's crazy-glued in there. Mr. Hoover carries Monica down to a chair that one of the stagehands has taken from the wings.

"Ice!" he calls out. "Somebody get some ice."

Someone's father who's a doctor has come onto the stage and looks at her ankle, which is already starting to swell.

"She needs an X-ray," he says. "As soon as possible. Keep it elevated."

"But the show . . ." says Monica's mother. "Sweetie, can you walk?"

Monica tries to put some weight on her foot, and she screams again. "The show's over," she says. "I can't finish."

"Oh, Monica," says her mother.

"Just tell everyone it's over," Monica says. "They all know what happens anyway. They've seen this stupid show a million times."

Meanwhile, Vijay manages to tug Monica's very high-heeled shoe out of the slats and he holds it out to Monica. She snatches it away and hands it to her mother.

I see Paul whispering something to Mr. Hoover and he nods and whispers back. Then he calls over Anita Messner, our wardrobe manager.

"Anita," I hear him say, "do we still have that other dress? The one with the garlic . . . I mean, tulip bulbs?" I don't get it. Why are they looking for the tulip dress? "I think it's in the instrument room. Can you pin it so it fits Shira?"

Suddenly I understand.

And so does Monica.

"Shira?" squeals Monica. "You want Shira to go on? Are you crazy?"

I find myself shaking my head. Actually, my head is shaking itself. And my mind is saying, "No, no, no, no, no."

"It's the end of the show!" Monica's still going. "It's over! And she doesn't even know the lines."

"Paul, Drew," Mr. Hoover calls. "Help Monica to the front, and let her take a bow."

"No! No, I can go on. I can." She tries to stand up but shrieks again.

"Monica, you're a trouper. We all know that," says Mr. Hoover in a gentle voice.

"Give me a break . . ." I hear Jason mutter, but he's too far away for me to elbow him.

"But you can't finish the show," continues Mr. Hoover. "You have to go to the hospital and get that X-ray. You gave a very fine performance, Monica. Don't worry about us. Go out and take your curtain call."

She blinks a few times, throws a piece of hair off her face, and sticks her chin out. "Well, of course I will," she says. Then she shoots me a quick glance and adds, "I guess it was lucky they kept the giant-size dress."

Paul and Drew prop Monica up between them. Actually, she clutches Drew around the neck with her head on his shoulder, and positions his hand around her waist, and Paul kind of dangles along on her right. Mr. Hoover whispers something to Dylan, then he follows Monica out.

"Okay, cast!" says Dylan. "We're going to do the rest of the show, but we need to chill for a few minutes. Everybody, stay where you are."

Out in the auditorium there's a lot of clapping, and then I hear Mr. Hoover's voice and then more applause for Monica. Soon Mr. Hoover is back behind the curtain and he comes straight over to me. "Shira," he says, putting his hands on my jacketed shoulders, "you can do it, can't you? You can be our Marian?"

The fact is, I know every word of the show. I've sung "Till There Was You" a hundred times up in my room. But that's not the same as being able to do it out there. What if it's like that time with Drew, and I can't sing at all?

I look down at my khaki pants and my jacket and bow tie. I'm Jacey Squires, first tenor in the barbershop quartet, member of the School Board of River City, Iowa. I'm Shira Gordon, who's never been a star of anything. How can I suddenly become Marian?

"Of course she can do it," says Paul, who's dumped

Monica off as soon as he could and run backstage. "Come on, Shira. Of course you can."

I can't answer. I feel my head doing that thing again. Shaking, no, no, no.

But then Cassie appears. "Come with me," she says, and suddenly I'm being dragged by my Jacey Squires lapel to a corner in the wings.

"Shira, I've had enough," she says.

"Enough what?"

"Enough of you not getting it. Everybody here knows you can do this. Everybody except you. How can you tell me to go out and do it, and then say you can't?"

"Because . . . because this is different. It's the lead role."

"So?"

"So, that's not me."

"Why not?"

"Because, I'm not."

"Not what? A star? Shira, what is wrong with you?! So, you're shy. Big deal. Stop hiding behind it. You can be shy and still be a star."

"You told me that. That day in the bathroom. But you also said girls with purple hair can be nobodies."

"They can. But I'm not. I proved it. Now it's your turn. Just go out there and show everybody what you can do. If you don't, what kind of waste is that?"

"But I don't know if—"

"Just be Marian. Everybody wants you to. And we're getting really tired of waiting."

I remember what Paul said, that day on the rock. You can't be shy when people are depending on you. I think about Felix, how I know a side of him that nobody else does. And there's Cassie. There's always Cassie.

"Can I go get the dress, please?" Cassie asks.

Over Cassie's shoulder, I see Vijay and Jason and Felix and Paul. They're all waiting. I take a deep breath.

"Okay," I say. "I'll do my best."

Cassie claps her hands and sends them all a thumbs-up, and Mr. Hoover smiles and pushes through the kids and out in front of the curtain again. I can hear him say, "Ladies and gentlemen, for the remainder of the show, the part of Marian will be played by Shira Gordon. Please bear with us for just a moment while we prepare to bring you the conclusion of Meredith Willson's *The Music Man*."

Cassie grabs me by the arm and pulls me through the back of the stage to the music room. She helps me peel off my sweaty jacket and shirt and pants and put on the dress, which is a little big, but it's not any huge size, no matter what Monica said. And the tulips are kind of pretty.

"Did you see Monica's face when she went out there for her bow?" Cassie says as she does the zipper in the back. "All that mascara and makeup running down her face? She looked like a linebacker after two overtimes."

"Maybe we should've told her."

"She's probably seeing it for herself right about now, in the car mirror." We look at each other and try not to smile.

"Quick, I have to do your makeup," says Johnny. He holds some mascara and stands poised for the attack on my eyelashes. Then he stops and stares at my face, horrified.

"What, it's no use?" I ask. He can't do it. He can't make me into something I'm not.

"No," he says. "No. It's . . . the mustache. We've got to get rid of the mustache."

I reach up and realize that I'm still wearing it. I pull at one side slowly, and Cassie says, "You have to do it all at once. Should I—"

"No. I'll do it." I shut my eyes and yank. It hurts and burns and I want to yell, but I hold it in.

"Uh-oh," says Johnny. "It's pretty red. We've got to cover that up." He puts pancake makeup over my red upper lip and lipstick on my lips and of course the mascara. Anita is frantically pinning the dress at the waist and in the back with safety pins, and Jenna Martinez is brushing my hair with a fury that practically takes my head off. I feel a little like Cinderella in the movie, when all the little birds work to get her ready for the ball. Maybe she should've warned us that it's not as easy as it looks. They sit me down and Cassie pulls off my Jacey Squires shoes and puts her ballet flats on me. I look down at her bare toes and think, *Pilgrim feet.* Finally, I get to look up in the mirror and I see . . . well, it's me, but another me. And coming from the mustached other me from the past two hours, it's a shock.

"Wow," I hear Cassie say behind me.

"You look amazing," says Johnny.

Just then Mr. Hoover sticks his head in. "Almost ready?" He comes in smiling, like it's just another rehearsal. "Look, I'll be right there, and Mrs. Highsmith can give you any cues you need." Mrs. Highsmith waves from behind him. I nod. "But I don't think you're going to need us."

He's turning away, but then he looks back at me. "By the way, have you noticed the trick with 'Goodnight, My Someone' and 'Seventy-Six Trombones'?"

"Trick?" I say. "You mean how Marian starts singing Harold Hill's song, and he sings Marian's?"

"Well, yes, but musically. Never mind. Just have fun out there."

Then he claps his hands and gets everyone's attention. "Okay, everybody! We're starting just before Marian comes out to meet Harold Hill. Paul, you're by the bridge, with Marcellus. Okay. Places, everyone."

Chapter 38

Bells on the Hill

Mr. Hoover has disappeared through the curtain and I can hear the audience quieting down. Paul takes his place by the bridge. He looks over and gives me a thumbs-up.

Mr. Hoover starts playing and the curtain starts to open. I listen to Paul's dialogue with Marcellus Washburn, waiting for my cue. Cassie and Vijay stand on either side of me, and Jason and Felix are a little farther behind.

I know the moment when I'm supposed to make my entrance. I hear Cassie's voice, saying "Go," and Vijay saying "Go on, Shira," but it's like my legs aren't working—one is shaking and the other is stuck to the floor. Mr. Hoover starts the four measures again. I know he can stall a long time without the audience catching on, but eventually I have to go out there.

"Come on, Marian," whispers Cassie. "Go meet Harold. He's waiting." Then I see her give a nod, and I feel a hand on my back and a not so soft push, and suddenly I find myself out on the stage.

There's nothing I can do but head toward the bridge. I keep my eyes on Paul and run to it, in Cassie's flats, and my tulip bulb dress. I can hear a few claps coming from the audience.

I've jumped the first hurdle, just making it up there in one piece.

"You're late," says Paul, and somehow, I remember what to answer. The dialogue is all about how late I am—Marian is—not only that night, but how late she is in meeting a "fella" on the footbridge at all. The words come out automatically, probably because of all those hours up in my room, practicing, saying those lines over and over just in case the Blue Marauder got his way and I ended up right where I am now, doing just what I'm doing.

My leg hasn't stopped shaking, and besides that, I can feel my heart beating. It's like somebody is using it like a punching bag. Luckily, I have the bridge railing to hold on to. Drew has sanded it to a perfect smoothness.

Then, somehow, we get to the end of the dialogue, and it's time for me to sing. There's no introduction, just a note that hangs in the air, waiting for me to pick it up and take it on its way. My mouth is dry, and I almost choke trying to swallow.

Cassie and the others must have scurried behind the stage, over to the other side, because now they're just yards from where I'm standing. They look so excited, waiting for me to start—Cassie grinning, Vijay next to her, and Felix with his wide-open eyes and his worried brow. Jason has his straw barbershop quartet hat on, and his fists clenched in front of him.

Mr. Hoover hits the note once more. I look at Paul and try not to think about the last time. How I froze and couldn't even start. This time, I start to sing.

There were bells on the hill, but I never heard them ringing,
No, I never heard them at all, till there was you.

It comes out, and I hear my own voice, and just like in the audition, it's the singing that calms me. This incredible melody that I can shape and move. It's hard to explain, but it's me and the music, and the music holds me up.

I take a few slow steps toward the middle of the bridge. When I get there, Paul takes my hands and I sing to him. With Paul, I look right into his eyes, and it feels different. I hear myself, and it sounds like Marian has finally said what she wanted to say all along.

Finally, at the end, Paul joins in and we sing the last lines together.

There was love all around, but I never heard it singing
No, I never heard it at all, till there was you.

It's a song about all the things I never did, all the music I didn't hear. I'm Marian the Librarian, singing to Harold Hill. But I'm Shira Gordon, too.

I hear the audience's applause and I look at Paul, and

that's when I realize, I'd forgotten all about the kiss. It's time for the kiss. I think maybe Paul will just leave it out because we're both too shy, and I'm not supposed to be here anyway. There are hundreds of people out there, and all our friends just a few feet away, and we haven't rehearsed it. But Paul kind of shrugs like "sorry, but it's in the script," and he puts his hands on my shoulders, and he kisses me.

The only problem is, the mustache glue on my upper lip isn't quite gone, and there's this sticky stuff between us, tugging at the little hairs above our lips. I hear Paul say "ow," and he pulls away, and I say "ow," too, and then we're both left rubbing our lips in front of everybody. The audience is laughing and clapping, and I feel myself blushing.

Over in the wings, Jason has taken his hat off and is hiding his face in it. Paul looks a little sheepish, but then we both start laughing, too. His big moment, my first kiss, in front of all those people, up in the spotlight, and that's how it goes.

There's one more scene change, and Cassie catches me in the wings and gives me a tight hug. I don't have time to be nervous, because I have to get back out there. There's one more song for Marian and Harold.

Marian is sitting on her porch, thinking about Harold, singing a reprise of "Goodnight, My Someone." Harold is on the other side of the stage. He's singing "Seventy-Six Trombones," but he knows that soon the whole town is going to be after him. He was, after all, trying to cheat everybody out of their money. But he's starting to realize that all these people are depending on him to bring music and instruments to their town for real. And he's also admitting to himself that he loves Marian. And Marian is starting to understand that Harold is more than a flimflam man, and she loves him, too. And she decides to stand up to everybody in River City and show them they're wrong about Harold Hill.

That's when Marian stops singing "Goodnight, My Someone" and switches to "Seventy-Six Trombones." And Harold Hill suddenly finds himself crooning "Goodnight, My Someone." And even though ninety-nine percent of me is focused on being here, up on stage in front of an auditorium full of people, some little part of my brain is puzzling out Mr. Hoover's comment. There's some musical trick about the two songs. Something he wants me to hear.

It's only when I make the switch, when I start singing "Seventy-Six Trombones," that I realize it.

It's the same melody—exactly the same notes. One song is slow and the other is fast, one is about love and the other is about crashing cymbals and trumpets. One is about wishing, the other is about going out there and grabbing it. But it's the same song.

I flash Mr. Hoover a look, and he smiles the most beautiful smile.

When we finish, the audience applauds, and we go on with the end of the show, with some chases and a few speeches, and then Harold Hill finally redeems himself when the boys' band somehow blats out a version of the Minuet in C. Then we all sing "Seventy-Six Trombones," and even though it's just Mr. Hoover on the piano, I could swear that there are drums and trumpets and trombones, as we march in place and sing the finale at the top of our lungs.

Before I know it, the crowd is cheering, and the curtain is coming down. We run to the wings to get arranged for the curtain call. Everyone is racing around, trying to get in order, and it seems like a second later that the curtain goes up and all the townspeople run out. Then comes Mrs. Shinn and her ladies, then Drew and Melinda, and suddenly, there out on the stage are Jason, Felix, and Vijay—the barbershop quartet.

I don't know what to do, but then I feel something on my head. It's my straw hat.

"Go on," says Cassie and I'm pushed—again—out onto the stage.

"Wait!" I call out, pushing in between Jason and Felix. We all bow in unison and the crowd cheers.

But as soon as we arrive back in the wings, Paul says, "Come on. There's still one to go." Cassie snatches the hat off of my head, and Paul slips his arm through mine. It feels strong and familiar, and he clutches me just tight enough to lead me out there, where everybody in the audience claps and cheers for us.

I can hear my father yelling "Brava, Shira," and I see Mr. Hoover grinning and Dr. Leeds waving and Mrs. Koch even puts her fingers in her mouth and whistles.

I soak it all in, but then after a minute, I unhook Paul's arm from mine, and this time I'm the one giving the push. Paul is at the front of the stage and I step back. And then the whole audience stands up for Paul, the Music Man, who brought a boys' band to River City, and River City to Hedgebrook Middle School, and to me.

Chapter 39

Crush

The music room is a mob scene. Everybody in the audience is family or friends, and everybody wants to go "backstage," so there isn't anywhere near enough room. We spill out into the hallway, and that's where I see my mother and father and Sophie.

"You were wonderful!" squeals my mother, practically knocking me over with a hug.

"I couldn't believe it," says my father. "You were like a pro. Called in at the last minute. I couldn't believe it."

"I would have thrown up," says Sophie.

"During the first act," says my mother, "I heard a lady behind me saying, 'Look at that little boy in the middle. Isn't he cute?' So I turned around and said, 'That's my daughter!'"

"She did, I heard her," mutters Sophie.

"And your voice was as clear as a bell," says my father.

"Beautiful," blubbers my mother.

Across the hall, I can see Drew with his parents. He shakes hands with his father, who puts his hand on Drew's head and messes up his hair.

"Harold Hill . . ." I hear Sophie say, and there's Paul, smiling at us, bouncing on his toes.

"Are these your parents?" he asks me.

"Yup," I say, "and my sister, Sophie."

"Hi, Sophie," says Paul, but Sophie just stares. "Wasn't Shira great?" He shakes my parents' hands.

"And you, too. You were marvelous!" My mother beams.

"Just wanted to say hi. My family's over there." He points and they wave energetically, his father, like a grown-up version of Paul, his mother, smiling wide, and his *abuela*, probably thinking about her Zarzuela days.

"Did you like the show, Sophie?" Paul asks.

Sophie nods. She looks awestruck. She's blushing, and more like a nine-year-old than I've seen her look in a long time.

"Well, nice to meet you, Mr. Gordon and Mrs. Gordon. Shira, I'll see you back onstage. Cast meeting." He runs off, back to his parents.

"Isn't he a nice boy!" says my mother.

"What's the matter?" I whisper to Sophie. "Got a crush?"

She glares at me, but she doesn't say no.

Then Mr. Donnelly comes bounding down the hallway. He grabs my hand and shakes it wildly. "Clutch," he says. "That was clutch. What a save, Shira. I've never seen anything like it."

"Thank you," I say, hoping that my hand isn't permanently squashed from his grip.

"Clear as a bell," my father is still saying.

I don't know how much more I can take. It's all wonderful, but my head is spinning. I'm grateful when Dylan comes around, tapping each cast member on the shoulder.

"Back on stage," he says. "We have to start striking the set and then there's a cast party. Come on, everybody," he calls out.

"I guess I've got to go," I say to my parents.

"We'll come get you later," says my mother.

"I don't know what time—" I start.

"It doesn't matter," says my father. "Any time you want."

We all say goodbye, and I hurry to the stage, where everyone is clustered around Mr. Hoover. There's already a feeling of nostalgia in the air, and I'm glad to be back on the stage. There's something alive about it, like it still holds all that energy from the past few hours.

"Okay, everybody, feel free to have a seat," says Mr. Hoover. Most kids stay standing, but all of a sudden, I feel like I can't stand for another minute, so I sit down on the stage floor.

"What can I say?" says Mr. Hoover, looking around at all of us. "That was . . . fantastic. Everybody, and I mean everybody came through." We all start clapping, and I can see that a few kids are looking at me. "You guys enjoy this.

You worked hard, you earned it. But listen, the night's not over. We need to get a jump on striking set. We'll move the big stuff tomorrow, but we should get started gathering up the props tonight."

"Strike the set," says Jason. "That sounds so dramatic."

"And we can celebrate, with some music and dancing, and some donuts, compliments of Dr. Leeds." Dr. Leeds makes a victory sign with both hands, and we actually give a cheer for the school psychologist.

It all sounds great to me. I'd stay here all night if I could.

"So, change and wash up, and Ms. Germano will collect your costumes. We'll meet back on stage when you're ready," says Mr. Hoover.

Everybody starts getting up and talking and moving in a hundred directions. Cassie and Vijay head toward the music room, Paul goes to check out Dr. Leeds's playlist, Felix and Jason start playing Frisbee with one of the straw hats. I just sit still, on the stage floor.

Then I look up, and I see Drew standing right in front of me.

"Hey," he says.

"Hey," I say back. He's already taken off his makeup and his hair is un-slicked, still a little wet, but hanging over his forehead like usual. For once, I manage to say exactly what I'm thinking. "You're already back to normal."

"Yeah. Ugh." He wipes his cheek and makes a face, like he hated it. The makeup, and maybe even more than that.

I realize that I'm still on the floor, but I can't quite figure out how to get up without stepping on the dress and falling down. It also occurs to me that Drew said hey to me and I answered him with an actual sentence.

"You going to Melinda's?" he asks me.

"Where?" I say.

"Melinda's," he says. "Her party." I look around for Melinda. The thought passes through my mind that maybe she sent Drew over to ask me as a joke and that she's watching from the wings to come out and laugh. But there's no sign of her.

"You mean after the cast party?" I ask.

"Huh?"

"The cast party," I say, wondering if I can stand up yet, but deciding not to risk it.

"Oh," he says. "With these kids. Huh." He looks around, and his upper lip crunches up, like he doesn't get it, why anyone would want to stay here with these kids a minute longer. "Nah," he says. "Melinda's invited some of us to her house. It'll be cool."

He holds out his hand and motions for me to take it. The tan rope bracelet circles his wrist. There's a little smudge of makeup on his right jawbone. He's inviting me to a party. Me, Shira. He knows who I am, and he wants me to go. With him. All I have to do is get up.

I try to make sure that I'm not standing on my dress. I wiggle my toes to make sure they aren't asleep. I try to cover all the bases that could make me end up back on the floor in a heap. Check, check, and check. Then I reach out, and Drew pulls me up, in one smooth motion. His hand feels warm and strong, and when I reach my feet, I'm standing so close, it's almost like dancing. And I know I'm blushing, but I don't mind. I think he is, too.

I point to that last spot of makeup. "You missed a spot." And instead of shaking with fear, I actually smile.

Drew wipes it off and rubs it on his jeans. "Come on," he says, still holding my hand. "You don't have to stick around here. Let's go."

Like Monica said, just because you're in a show with people doesn't mean you have to hang out with them.

I look around. Vijay is posing by the sign that says "Ewart Dunlop, Staples & Fancy Groceries" as Cassie takes his picture. Jason is teetering on a chorus room chair, which Felix is threatening to pull out from under him. He's taking down the sign that says "Oliver Hix." I look for Paul, but I don't know where he's gone.

I look at Drew, and I gently pull my hand back from his.

"Thanks, but I'm going to stay here," I say. He looks a little puzzled. "It's kind of a thing with friends."

Drew looks around at the kids on the stage. It probably doesn't look to him like much of a scene to hang around for. He shrugs. "Okay," he says.

"But, thanks," I say. "Really."

He shrugs again and I watch him hop down the stairs and down the aisle. Melinda meets him there, and then they're gone.

I stand there for a minute, then look over to see Jason taking down the sign that says "Jacey Squires, Blacksmith." He hands it to Felix, who hasn't pulled the chair out from under him after all.

"Hey!" I call out. "Save that sign for me, okay?"

"You got it, Oh-and-Shira," says Jason. "You got it."

I start toward the music room to take off my fluffy garlic dress and put on my jeans and T-shirt.

But before I can get very far, Cassie comes up beside me and says, "Shira, wait. I have to tell you something." After everything that's happened, I don't know what else anyone could have to tell me.

But it's Cassie, so I stop and listen.

"Shira," she says. "Remember that day when you went to see Donnelly?"

"Of course I do," I say, wondering why she would possibly be talking about that now. "The day we got Paul off the hook."

"Right. So remember how Vijay didn't go with you?"

"Vijay? Yeah. Of course."

"Well, it was because of me."

"I know. He went to back you up, in the guidance office—"

"But it was more than that." Cassie smiles. "He wanted to tell me that he liked me."

"He did?"

"Yes. Well, no. I mean, yes, he did like me, but no, he didn't get up the nerve to tell me that day. We just talked about stuff. We had a really good time, but I didn't think anything about it. But before, when he said he thought I looked—"

"Beautiful," I fill in.

"Yeah," she says, holding in a grin. "He just told me he's been wanting to say that for months. And the thing is, I like him, too."

"Cassie," I say, "that's great!" I grab her and hug her, and I'm not surprised at all.

"So, go change. I'll tell Vijay I told you, so he can tell his friends, too. And Shira . . ."

"Yeah?"

"You're such a star."

"So are you, Cassie," I say, and I hug her again. Even though I barely avoid getting poked in the eye by her huge, wing-shaped earring, she feels squishy and warm and safe.

Cassie watches as I take one last spin, to enjoy the

ruffles and admire my purple tulips. Then I go wash up and change.

When I come back onstage, parts of the sets are already dismantled. It's sad, almost, to see it all gone so soon.

Vijay stands next to Cassie, grinning. Felix and Jason are taking down a part of the Paroos' porch. I look out into the auditorium seats. They're empty now, but I remember how they'd looked just an hour before.

Suddenly, the music starts, and Dylan announces that he's opening the donut boxes. Everyone starts crowding around, reaching in to get their favorites, but I don't see Paul. I check back in the music room, and then in both wings. Then, finally, I see him, standing in a shadowy spot near the front of the stage. He's looking out into the empty auditorium. I come up behind him.

"You were great," I say.

"You were awesome," he answers.

"I'm sorry it's over."

"Me too."

Behind us, Dylan turns up the music.

"Are you going to Melinda's?" he asks softly.

"What? No. Are you?"

"Me?" he says. "No. Of course not."

"Well, neither am I. Why would I want to go to Melinda's?"

"But before . . . I saw you with Drew. I thought . . ."

"Did you really think I would miss the cast party?"

"I don't know. It's just that—"

"Not in a million years."

Then, because it's a night of changes and firsts, and because I've been thinking about it, and I know if I wait I'll chicken out, I say quickly, "Do you want to dance?"

And Paul smiles. We're the first ones, but soon we're surrounded by the rest of the cast. Everybody joins in. The music is loud, and we all jump and sing along. I raise my hands over my head and bump hips with Cassie and Vijay, Felix, Jason, and Paul. We're all out there together, wishing it would never end. And I dance with my dozens of friends, on the stage of Hedgehog Middle School, until midnight.

Chapter 40

AKA Marian

On Monday, more people talk to me than have talked to me in all of the other days I've been at school put together. Kids I don't even know tell me how awesome we were, and teachers I haven't even had smile and say "Great job."

At lunch, kids keep passing by our table, telling us how great the show was. Paul gets so many pats on the back, he can hardly eat his lunch. Some kids even say they want to be in the show next year. But regular middle school life goes on. Cassie complains that she's stuck with meal worm habitat cleanup in science, and I warn them all about the pop quiz in math. Ms. Jablonski doesn't care about big games or science expos or musicals.

"Pop quizzes are unfair," complains Jason, who also has first-period math. "They're pop for the first-period kids, but they're not pop for anyone else."

Lunch is almost over, and Felix is searching through his backpack. "I think I left my English notebook in my locker." His brow is wrinkled. The six of us always walk together to sixth period.

"I'll go with you," I say. I can stash *How We Remember* back in my locker.

"We'll catch up with you," calls Cassie.

Felix and I hurry to our lockers. We're just ahead of the flood of seventh graders leaving lunch and the torrent of eighth graders going in.

"I don't know what I'll do with myself without rehearsal after school," says Felix. "I might have to take up shot put or pole vault or something."

I'm about to answer, when we practically walk right into Monica.

She's leaning on a pair of crutches, with Melinda at her side. She holds her leg out in front of her, with her brand-new, bright pink cast. A group of sixth graders clusters excitedly around to sign it. "Shira," says Monica, looking up. "I've been looking for you."

"I'll see you," mutters Felix, drifting off to his locker, leaving me alone to face Monica and her posse.

I gulp and take a few steps closer and look at her cast. It's already covered with names and smiley faces in multi-colored markers. I'm not sure what to say. "How was your weekend?" certainly isn't going to work.

"How are you feeling?" I try. "Does that . . . hurt?"

"Not as much as yesterday," she says. "It itches mostly. But it's waterproof, so I can shower. That was the first thing I said, I need a waterproof cast, in pink."

"Great," I say.

"So, you have to sign it." Monica signals to Melinda, who holds out a baggie filled with markers. Monica picks out a turquoise one and hands it to me. She shoos away the sixth graders, who scatter like sparrows, and I crouch down to find an empty space to write my name.

"Seventh graders are on this side." She turns her leg a little sideways, and I have to twist to find an empty pink space. I write my name, and I'm about to hand back the marker, but she says, "Wait. Put 'AKA' and the name of the guy you played. Kids from the show are signing it that way, with their part from the play. 'AKA,' it's Latin or something."

I wonder if I should tell her that it stands for "also known as," but I decide just to write "AKA Jacey Squires."

"Oh, and Shira," she says. I look up. "Also write 'AKA Marian.' 'Marian the Librarian' if it'll fit."

"But—" I start.

"Just write it." She looks like she did at our first rehearsal, like I'm totally hopeless and she wonders why she should even bother.

I write "AKA Marian the Librarian" and look up at her and our eyes meet. For just a second, I can almost imagine that she's, in some Monica way, proud of me.

I hear some laughter down the hall. It's coming from a group of boys. One of them is Drew.

Monica waves, and before I know it, she's speed-limping down the hall at an impressive rate calling, "Hey, Drew, sign my cast!" All it takes is the right goal, I guess. She's over there in a flash, holding out her leg for all of them to admire. Melinda snatches the marker out of my hand and follows behind Monica. I watch for a second, long enough to see Drew signing right down by her pink polished toenails.

I head to my locker. Felix is waiting for me, busy taping the *Music Man* program to the inside of his locker door, a few down from mine.

"That's some cast, huh?" he says as I fish *How We Remember* out of my backpack.

"Pink," I say.

"How long does she have to have it on?"

"I didn't ask." I shut my locker, spin the lock, and walk over to Felix. "By the way," I whisper. "I've been wondering. How exactly did the Blue Marauder do it, with the costumes?"

Felix smiles. "Ms. Channing gave him the forms to take to the office, remember? He just changed it . . . a little bit."

"But the Blue Marauder is retired, right?"

"Absolutely." Then he reaches up to the top shelf of his locker. "But I kept a souvenir." In his hand is Monica's Jade Marimba Teal.

"Felix! Put that away!"

"Okay, okay. But, I'm thinking maybe I should buy Monica a new one. A new Jade. I feel kind of bad, like I should even things up." He looks down at the eyeliner in his hand, then up at me. "I could get a new one and just slip it into her bag one day. What do you think?"

What do I think? I think he should just put it away. I think he should forget there ever was a Blue Marauder. But I look at his troubled face, and I picture Monica's, if a brand-new Jade just suddenly appeared in her bag. So, I just sigh and say, "Let me know if you need backup."

Just then, Vijay and Cassie come around the corner, with Jason and Paul behind them.

"What's taking you so long?" asks Jason.

"I had to sign Monica's cast," I say.

"She let you?" asks Cassie.

"She made me," I say. "And then Felix and I were talking about the Blue Marauder." We start down the hallway together, toward our sixth-period classes. "Do you think we'll ever find out who it was?"

"Maybe someday," says Cassie.

"Paul, are you sure it wasn't you?" I say.

"Me?" He stops and stares at me. "Yes, I'm sure it wasn't me."

"Mr. Hoover?" says Cassie.

Suddenly I realize that Felix is still holding Monica's Jade in his left hand. He's forgotten all about it.

"Hey, Felix," I say. "Can I borrow that pen?" Felix looks down at the Jade in his hand and his eyes open wide. I'm afraid he's going to fling it in the air like a grenade with the pin pulled, but before he can, I snatch it and stuff it in my backpack. "Thanks," I say, giving him a grin. "It's nice to have friends when you need them."

"Sure." Felix lets out a little puff of air that only I notice.

"I guess we'll never find out," says Vijay.

"Maybe it's better that way," says Paul. "Some things are best unknown."

"The tale will live on as Hedgehog legend." I shoot Felix a look.

"Or maybe next year, the Blue Marauder will return," Jason's voice booms out.

"I hope he doesn't have to," I say.

"Or she," adds Cassie.

And we talk, dawdling our way to class, not wanting to split up just yet. And the afternoon sun shines its spotlights on all of us.

Acknowledgments

When I was nine years old, I played Jacey Squires in a summer school production of *The Music Man* at E. M. Baker Elementary School. I'd like to acknowledge my music teacher, the late Mr. Ron Howard, for his creative casting, for his belief in what kids can accomplish, and for giving me a starting point for *Upstaged*. I'd also like to extend my thanks to every dedicated and talented music teacher who brings the excitement of musical theater to their students.

Thanks to Nicole James for always being in my corner, and to my gifted editor, Erica Finkel, for her patience and encouragement. I'm grateful to everyone at Abrams for once again supporting me and believing in my storytelling. Thanks to Steven Schnur, Alyssa Capucilli, and my classmates at the Sarah Lawrence Writing Institute for their encouragement as I began this book; to MacKenzie Cadenhead and Jessica Benjamin, who are always there to give me a push when I need it; and to Debra Tanklow, who shared some of the secrets of putting on a student performance.

I grew up in a home filled with love and music, so I owe this book and so much more to my mother, my father, and my sister, Marcie.

As always, all my love and thanks to Henry, Bobby, Adam, Benjy, and my beautiful brand-new daughter-in-law, Catherine, for being such a precious part of my life. And to Cassie Wangsness (who made her entrance after Cassie was already named Cassie) and Christy Serwon, thank you for adding your charm and kindness to all of our lives.

And finally, I want to thank all the young readers, parents, teachers, librarians, and booksellers for their warm and wonderful reception of my first novel, *Sidetracked*. I've loved every letter, every email, and every school visit. It has been a joy and an honor to be part of your reading and running lives.

About the Author

Diana Harmon Asher is the author of *Sidetracked*, the mother of three sons, and the daughter of two gifted singers. Her own first singing role was in a summer school production of *The Music Man*, when she played Jacey Squires. She lives with her husband, Henry, and their dog, Cody, and cat, Chester, in Westchester, New York.

The following songs have been reproduced with permission: